"Why wouldn't my sister want us to get together and share life with her?" Rick asked

"Lindy is so young—she's still just a child. What if she fears I may not care for her as much as I did, because I'm in love with you?" Vanessa replied.

"Are you?"

"Am I what?"

"In love with me?"

Vanessa felt her cheeks burn and she looked away. She wouldn't answer his question. She couldn't. Instead she took a different approach. "Rick, I've worked for four years on my advanced degree. I have six more months of work. Then I'll be able to pursue a career I love."

"Okay," he said with a sigh. "Six months isn't forever." *It just seems like forever when I want to marry you now!*

Dear Reader,

We've come to the end of the CHILDREN OF TEXAS series. In the first four books Vanessa played a secondary role to her sisters' and brother's stories, and has been patiently waiting for her time in the sun.

As the youngest of the Barlow family, Vanessa had to grow up a bit before she was ready for her own story. In the meantime, she, along with Will and Vivian, looked for and found her other siblings. Each one was brought into the family and made to feel a part of it. The family has grown and babies have appeared.

Though Vanessa loves her siblings, and their babies even more, she has been lonesome at times because she didn't have anyone special for herself. I wanted Vanessa to have her reward, but, as we all know, no reward really fills a void unless you work for it. I hope you'll cheer on Vanessa through her struggles, and share in her happiness at the end.

It's been a pleasure to bring you this family and all of its stories. I hope that you, too, have a family to share with. But remember, family doesn't have to be of the same blood. Just reach out to those around you whom you love—and form your own family.

If you have any comments or questions, you can reach me at my Web site, www.judychristenberry.com.

Happy reading!

Judy Christenberry

Judy Christenberry

VANESSA'S MATCH

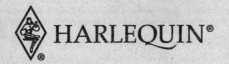

HARLEQUIN®

TORONTO • NEW YORK • LONDON
AMSTERDAM • PARIS • SYDNEY • HAMBURG
STOCKHOLM • ATHENS • TOKYO • MILAN • MADRID
PRAGUE • WARSAW • BUDAPEST • AUCKLAND

ISBN 0-373-75121-4

VANESSA'S MATCH

This edition published by arrangement with Harlequin Books S.A.

® and TM are trademarks of the publisher. Trademarks indicated with
® are registered in the United States Patent and Trademark Office, the
Canadian Trade Marks Office and in other countries.

www.eHarlequin.com

Printed in U.S.A.

ABOUT THE AUTHOR

Judy Christenberry has been writing romances for over fifteen years because she loves happy endings as much as her readers do. A former French teacher, Judy now devotes herself to writing full-time. She hopes readers have as much fun with her stories as she does. She spends her spare time reading, watching her favorite sports teams and keeping track of her two daughters. Judy lives in Texas.

Books by Judy Christenberry

HARLEQUIN AMERICAN ROMANCE

*Brides for Brothers
†Tots for Texans
**Children of Texas

Don't miss any of our special offers. Write to us at the following address for information on our newest releases.

Harlequin Reader Service
U.S.: 3010 Walden Ave., P.O. Box 1325, Buffalo, NY 14269
Canadian: P.O. Box 609, Fort Erie, Ont. L2A 5X3

Prologue

"I need your help."

Even through the haze of sleep, Vanessa Shaw recognized the voice that woke her at— She focused with difficulty on the bedside clock. Two a.m. Why was Dr. Cavanaugh calling her now? He was the head of the Psychology Department and Vanessa's supervisor in her quest for her doctorate of psychology. For him to phone in the middle of the night, she knew the matter must be urgent.

"Yes, Dr. Cavanaugh, what is it?" she asked, clutching the phone with one hand and rubbing her eyes with the other.

"Sorry to wake you, Vanessa, but I need you."

"Of course. Anything I can do." One didn't say no to Dr. Cavanaugh, even at two a.m.

Her mentor took her at her word and, without pausing, launched into an explanation. "There's a fifteen-year-old girl in the hospital right now having her stomach pumped. She attempted suicide following her mother's death in a car accident. The family attorney called and asked me to supply someone to be with her when she awoke and to help her through this tragedy." Not waiting for a comment, he continued. "You're the most senior female in the program, and a very good student. I've seen your work with some desperate cases, so I immediately thought of you."

Vanessa sat up. Surely he didn't expect her to fill the role he'd described. "Thank you, sir, but—"

"She's part of the Austin family."

It was a name she recognized instantly. The Austins had donated millions to the university.

"I don't have to tell you how important this family is to the university." The doctor's voice deepened. "Or to your future."

It wasn't a threat; it didn't have to be. Vanessa knew what she had to do.

She cleared her throat. "Yes, sir, I'll be right there."

Chapter One

Vanessa smiled as her patient, Lindy Austin, played with Vanessa's niece, Jamie. Turning two and sweet as spun sugar, Jamie made Lindy laugh as they played with the plastic dollhouse and the toddler babbled on. Vanessa suspected it had been a while since Lindy had laughed like that.

Ever since she'd received the call that sent her to the hospital in the middle of the night five days ago, Vanessa had taken care of Lindy, and eventually brought her here to her mother's house in the Highland Park section of Dallas, where Vanessa still lived. Lindy had said she couldn't face going back to the condo she'd lived in with her mother.

Only Vanessa had gone to the condo to pack some clothes for Lindy. And she'd been disturbed by what she'd found. Richard Austin, Lindy's half brother, had a lot to answer for. At the time of the accident he'd been in Japan on business and had ordered his attorney to make sure Lindy was taken care of. That had been the extent of Richard's involvement. Because of the Austins' connections to the university Dr. Cavanaugh got involved, but he knew little about Richard Austin.

Vanessa had so many questions about the man. But she couldn't ask Lindy. The teen reacted badly to the mere mention of his name, which made Vanessa even more determined to protect the girl. How, she wasn't sure, but she'd find a way.

"Vanessa?" Betty, the housekeeper, came into the morning room, breaking into her thoughts.

Vanessa looked up quickly. There was a hint of urgency in the housekeeper's voice that alarmed her.

"What is it, Betty?"

"You have a caller. Shall I show him to the library?"

Vanessa paused. She started to ask the name of the visitor, but Betty's gaze darted to Lindy and then back to Vanessa. So the caller was about her charge. "Yes, thank you."

She looked at her sister, Jamie's mom. "I've been expecting this visitor. Rebecca, can you keep an eye on everyone for a few minutes?"

She was glad Rebecca was here. There was a special bond between the sisters, perhaps because Rebecca was the first of her siblings found a couple of years ago. Not a day went by that Vanessa didn't thank her mother, Vivian Greenfield, for telling her that she was adopted and offering to help Vanessa find her siblings. Four out of the five had been located, with the help of Will Greenfield, a private investigator and Vivian's second husband. The last sibling would never be found: Walter Barlow, a soldier, had been killed in Iraq.

For being a devoted mother and for understanding Vanessa's need to find her siblings, she would forever love her mother. Brothers and sisters had enriched her life immeasurably.

Too bad that wasn't the case for young Lindy.

Vanessa gave her sister a thankful nod when she agreed. As the mother of two, Rebecca would do anything to protect Lindy, too, Vanessa knew. "I'll hurry back," she said.

Vanessa left the morning room and went to the library. She entered the room quietly, but she didn't catch her visitor by surprise.

He turned and studied her. "Are you Vanessa Shaw?"

"Yes, I am." When he said nothing else, she spoke up. "My housekeeper didn't mention your name."

"I'm Richard Austin, here to pick up my sister."

Even his voice was cold.

Vanessa took a good look at the man she'd been obsessing about since she'd met his sister. He was tall, and dressed impeccably in what looked like a custom-made Italian suit. His dark hair had that just-cut look, and something made her believe it always did. The chill that radiated from his dark eyes came as no surprise to her. The man would never ease Lindy's fears.

Keeping her reaction under wraps, she effected a

professional distance, slowly walked over to the fireplace and sat down in one of the wing chairs. "Well, then, Mr. Austin, would you join me, please? I'd like to talk to you about Lindy."

"There's no need. Just bring the girl to me. I'm in a hurry."

Vanessa said nothing, just stared at him.

Finally, he moved to the other wing chair. "Make it quick."

Vanessa grew more determined. She couldn't possibly hand Lindy over to this ice man. "What are your plans for Lindy?"

"I'll return her to the condo and find a responsible person to take care of her."

"But you won't concern yourself with her?" Vanessa asked.

"What are you getting at? The girl is a stranger to me."

Without knowing, he was making her case for her. "And whose fault is that? According to Lindy, you're always too busy even to talk to her."

"That's none of your business, Miss Shaw."

"I think it is. I was at the hospital with her when she came to, after attempting to commit suicide. I've taken care of her for the past five days while you were too busy to find out how she was doing."

"What do you mean she tried to commit suicide?" he demanded, frowning deeply.

"No one told you?"

"No!"

"She was alone when she was notified that her mother had been killed. Emotionally distraught, she swallowed her mother's sleeping pills and almost died. Fortunately, your lawyer realized that might be a difficult blow to a fifteen-year-old and came to the apartment to see if she was all right."

"Why didn't he tell me?" Richard demanded, jumping to his feet.

"Perhaps he was afraid of displeasing you." Her father had been an important businessman like the one in front of her, and he'd generated fear among his employees and everyone around him, no doubt like Richard did. Vanessa had learned to overcome that fear and had faced her adoptive father many a time. She would do the same with Richard Austin. She had to, for Lindy's sake.

The man scowled at her. "Never mind. Bring Lindy to me."

"So she can become distraught and try to kill herself again?" She wasn't going to pull her punches.

"I said I'd find someone to take care of her!" he snapped.

"Leave her with me."

She could see that she had caught him by surprise with that request.

"I beg your pardon?"

"Leave your sister here with me. I have room for her and I care about her."

"She has a perfectly good condo to go to!"

"Have you been to the condo?"

He scowled again. "Once, when I bought it for them."

"Well, let me tell you about the place she called home. I went to pack up Lindy's clothes when she came to stay with me. The living room is beautifully decorated, the master bedroom lovely, the dining room elegant." She speared him with a look. "But there's no table in the kitchen, and Lindy slept on a pallet on the floor. Her clothes are few and cheap, but the master bedroom has a closet full of designer clothes and shoes. Whose fault is that?"

He came back to his chair and sank into it. "I left her with her mother, who had legal custody. What else should I have done?"

"Perhaps you could have visited occasionally. It wasn't just you who lost your father. Lindy did, too."

"You don't understand!"

"Then tell me what I don't understand," she said softly.

"The damn woman tried to seduce me two days after we buried my father."

"And you left Lindy with that kind of woman?" she demanded.

"She was her mother!" the man roared.

Vanessa drew a deep breath. "Please control yourself, Mr. Austin."

"I damn well won't if you're going to keep accusing me of doing something wrong!"

"Couldn't you at least have made sure she had the necessities?"

"The money I paid out each month was double what they were entitled to."

"Well, now you can save all that money. Just leave Lindy with me. She needs a lot of love and protection right now for her to recover."

Silence.

"You do want her to recover, don't you?"

"Of course I do. But I know nothing about you."

"At least you don't know anything bad about me. You can't say that about the woman you left her with nine years ago."

"Do you have any references?" he demanded, starch in his voice.

"Yes, Dr. Cavanaugh, head of the Psychology Department. He sent me to the hospital. He'll vouch for me."

"Very well. I'll contact him. If I agree to this arrangement, the two of you can move into the condo. I'll make sure it's furnished this time."

"No."

"What do you mean, no?"

"I want Lindy to stay here with me, where she'll feel like she's in a family."

"A big house does not a family make, Miss Shaw."

"My parents, my baby brother, the housekeeper

and her husband live here. I also have two brothers and a sister nearby. In fact, my sister is here now with her two-year-old. Lindy is enjoying playing with her."

"That would be an imposition. I'll find someone to take care of her."

"No!" Vanessa exclaimed, jumping to her feet. "I insist that you leave Lindy here. She's not strong enough to be on her own."

He paused, frowning. Then he said, "I suppose I could pay you for her upkeep and your care of her, if I decide it will be the best thing for her."

"If you'll leave her here, I won't charge you anything."

"I insist. I don't believe in owing anyone."

"Whatever—as long as you leave her here."

"All right, I'll let you know my decision after I make some calls. Here's my card. If you need anything for Lindy in the meantime, let me know at once."

"Thank you. Will you inform your lawyer?"

"Of course…after I speak to him about not telling me the truth about Lindy."

With that, he was gone.

WHAT'S WRONG WITH ME? I spilled my guts! Rick Austin drove too fast as he left, his mind focused on the conversation he'd just had with the beautiful Miss Shaw.

He hadn't told anyone about Anita's behavior after his father's death. He hadn't explained to anyone, except to Anita, why he had moved his stepmother and his little sister out of the family home and into a condo. He'd had no intention of ever seeing his step-mother again.

It was something that had gnawed at his soul since his father's death. He'd hated Anita from the first day his father had brought her home. She was a gold digger of the highest order and she was replacing his mother? He couldn't believe his father could be so blind.

From that moment, his relationship with his father had been ruined. He'd moved out and found his own place as soon as he could, but he'd continued to work with his father because he understood that it was his job, as well as his desire, to learn how to juggle the various companies his father owned. One day he would be responsible for maintaining the Austin Group, the corporation that controlled all the companies.

At the office, his father had never challenged him about his attitude toward Anita. Which had made him feel guilty, but not enough so to do anything about it. By the time Lindy was born, he thought his father had realized the kind of woman Anita was, but it was too late. Rick knew his father would never give up Lindy.

Which was exactly what he himself had done as soon as his father died and Anita had shown her true colors.

Damn! He hated having to admit what he'd done. He hadn't wanted to have anything to do with the woman who had ruined his happy family. He'd adored his mother, and he and his father had mourned her passing. For a year or so after her death, they'd been closer than ever.

Then Anita had entered the family.

In his anger and disgust, Rick hadn't realized he was isolating himself from his half sister. She was only six years old, a cute kid, but he figured she'd grow up and be like her mother.

Suddenly he turned his car in the direction of the condo. He had to see if what Miss Shaw had said was true. He grabbed his cell phone and hit the button to automatically dial his lawyer, Joe Adderly. After two rings, Joe picked up.

"Joe? It's Rick Austin."

"Yes, Rick. What can I do for you?"

"Meet me at the condo, and bring the key."

"Yes, sir. I'll be right there."

And he would, because Rick paid him a lot of money to be at his beck and call. One of Joe's jobs had been to keep an eye on Lindy. At least Rick had done that much, though it hadn't been much for a six-year-old. Rick now knew his lawyer hadn't done a good job. But then, neither had he.

His lips tightened into a line as anger grew in him. He'd instructed his lawyer to visit Anita and Lindy once a month to give them the check and be sure Lindy was properly cared for. And to let Rick know if she wasn't. He'd never heard a word from the man.

He screeched to a halt in front of the condo. Good, he'd arrived before Joe. He got out of his car and went upstairs to the second floor. But the condo was locked. He snickered. Joe had found his half sister on the verge of death but he hadn't forgotten to lock the door.

Rick heard footsteps. He turned to watch Joe climb the stairs, a smile on his face.

"Hi, Rick. I didn't even realize you were in town yet."

"Really? How's Lindy?"

"She's fine," the man said heartily.

"Where is she?"

"She's still in the hospital. She's going to be fine, of course, but they wanted to make sure."

"I see. Would you unlock the door?"

"Yes, of course."

The man stepped forward and inserted a key into the lock.

As he did so, Rick said, "And you visited the condo each month and saw Lindy?"

"Yes, and she was doing fine. I think it was just the shock of her mother's death that upset her."

"Why was she alone? Didn't they have a house-keeper?"

"Yes, I believe they did. I didn't think to ask— Well, who would I ask, after all? Lindy was in no shape for any conversation."

"Of course." Rick stepped through the door of the condo and saw what Miss Shaw had seen. A beauti-fully decorated living room. A dining room table and chairs that looked like it had never been used. He walked through to the kitchen and again, as she'd said, there was no table.

The lawyer followed along silently.

Next, Rick went to the master bedroom. It, too, was elaborately decorated. Rick opened the large closet and looked at some of the designer labels.

Joe smiled at him.

Then Rick turned to the second bedroom. After he walked through the door, he moved aside for the lawyer and folded his arms over his chest.

Joe gasped and turned to stare at Rick. "I—I don't know what happened to the furniture in here!"

"What furniture?"

"Well, surely there was furniture. It's Lindy's bedroom, after all."

"Have you ever seen Lindy's bedroom before?"

"Well, no, of course not. I mean—it wouldn't have been proper for me to go into her bedroom."

"But you saw Lindy every time you brought over the check?"

"Absolutely!"

"And you've visited her in the hospital?"

"Of course, every day. I sometimes took my lunch hour and spent it with Lindy."

"When was the last day you spent with Lindy in the hospital?"

"Why…yesterday, of course."

Rick pulled out his cell phone and dialed the number he'd been given for Vanessa Shaw. He recognized the housekeeper's voice when she answered. "May I speak to Vanessa Shaw, please?"

Joe was frowning.

"Miss Shaw? Rick Austin. Did you meet my attorney while you were at the hospital with Lindy?" He waited for her response, his gaze on the attorney. "And you were with her all the time?

"How long did she remain in the hospital? I see. Thank you, Miss Shaw."

He hung up and turned to look at his attorney. "Joe, the woman who has been taking care of Lindy says she never saw you at the hospital." The man started to answer and Rick held up a hand to stop him. "She also said Lindy left the hospital four days ago, so think before you tell any more lies."

"I thought— I tried to do as you asked, but Mrs. Austin always said Lindy was out."

"What time did you usually come over?"

"She asked that I come over around two."

Rick put his hands on his hips and shook his head. "Joe, I didn't think you were that dumb. Lindy was in school at two every afternoon, unless you came over on a Saturday."

"I'm sorry. I—I made a mistake. It won't happen again."

"And how often have you lied to me in the past nine years?"

"Never about business, Rick. I swear!"

"Our relationship, business and otherwise, is over,

Joe. I'll let you know my new attorney's name so you can send the files to him."

"Rick, you can't do this to me. It will ruin me."

"You should've thought of that before you lied to me and failed to do what I asked. My little sister has been living in poverty while her mother was leading the high life! That wasn't what I wanted, and I believe I made myself clear."

Rick held out his hand for the key and stood waiting while his ex-attorney struggled to undo his key ring. While Joe did so, he pleaded for another chance, but Rick ignored him.

Once he had the key in his hand, Rick led him outside the condo, locked the door and pocketed the key. Without a word he walked away, Joe still trying to apologize and regain his trust.

After getting into his car without waving goodbye, Rick returned to the house where he'd left Vanessa Shaw. He felt he owed her an apology.

When he rang the doorbell, Betty recognized him at once and invited him in. She was leading the way to the library when another door opened and Vanessa Shaw came out with a young girl.

Rick stopped and stared. Could this slender blond lady be his half sister? "Lindy?"

The girl stared at him. Then, without a word, she crumpled to the floor.

Chapter Two

"What's wrong with her?" For an instant Rick was frozen in place, then he rushed over to Lindy, about five yards away. Vanessa, he noticed, had reacted immediately and was cradling the girl in a maternal gesture.

"She's been worried about your return. I didn't tell her about your earlier visit. She wasn't ready for it." She pushed Lindy's hair out of her face with a caring touch. "What are you doing here again?"

"I needed to talk to you."

"You're not going to take her away, are you?" Vanessa demanded sharply.

"No, not now."

"Then go into the library. I'll join you when I can." She called out to Betty, who appeared almost instantly. "Will you help me get her upstairs?"

"A' course," Betty agreed. "That poor child."

"I could carry her wherever you're taking her," Rick suggested.

Vanessa shook her head. "I'm afraid she'll wake up and you will frighten her all over again."

The front door opened then and a middle-aged man stepped inside. "Hi—What's going on?" he demanded.

Vanessa greeted him with gratitude. "Thanks for coming home now, Will. Could you carry Lindy upstairs?"

"Sure." He frowned. "Is she sick?"

"No, just a little overwhelmed. Betty, will you come with us? Mr. Austin, you know the way to the library, don't you? I'll be down in a minute."

The trio, with Lindy, disappeared up the stairs.

Rick turned and went into the library. He left the door open so that he could hear Miss Shaw come in.

"Hello?" a sweet voice said.

He turned around to find an attractive woman staring at him. "Uh, hello. I'm waiting to see Miss Shaw."

"Oh. I'm her mother, Vivian Greenfield." The petite woman crossed the room to shake his hand. "I don't believe I've met you."

Feeling like a gauche schoolboy, Rick hurriedly said, "I'm Rick Austin."

"Oh, are you any kin to Lindy?"

"Yes, ma'am. I'm her half brother."

"Then I'm glad to meet you. We've enjoyed having Lindy stay here."

"I hope—"

"What are you doing talking to my mother?"

Vanessa Shaw demanded, making it sound as if doing so were a heinous crime.

The man who had carried Lindy upstairs entered behind her and patted her on the back. "Easy, Vanessa."

"Yes, dear, why wouldn't I talk to one of our guests?" Mrs. Greenfield asked.

"Because, Mom, he's the one who abandoned Lindy for nine years."

"I thought my lawyer would take care of everything!" Rick exclaimed. "Now that I've found out how careless he was, how much he lied to me, I've fired him."

"Too bad," Miss Shaw returned with heavy sarcasm.

"Would you stop ripping me up? I explained what happened. I left her with her mother."

"Yes, because she had so much character!"

The middle-aged woman stepped forward. "Darling, I don't think you're giving him a chance."

"I don't see why I should!" Vanessa retorted.

Before tempers flared further Will told them all to sit down. Then he introduced himself to Rick. "I'm Will Greenfield, and this is my wife, Vivian, who is Vanessa's mother. I gather you're the half brother we've been waiting for?"

"Yes. I wasn't told that Lindy had tried to kill herself. And my lawyer was instructed to visit with Lindy each month when he delivered the check, to be sure she was doing all right. I told him to let me

know if there were any problems. Since I never heard
from him…" He paused, staring at Vanessa. "I'll
admit I should've checked things out, but my stepmother had…had made it impossible for me to visit
in her household."

"She made a pass at him," Vanessa said calmly.

"How old were you at the time, Rick?" Will asked.

"Twenty-two. My father had just died and I was
off balance as it was. My response to her attempt to
seduce me—which was more than a pass, Miss
Shaw—was to get as far away from her as possible."

"You should've fought for custody of Lindy,"
Vanessa interjected.

"I didn't have a choice about that. My father made
me her guardian in the will only if I survived her
mother. All I controlled was the money."

Vanessa pressed on. "Well, you certainly could
have used the money as leverage, couldn't you?"

"Vanessa, that's not really your business," her
mother said gently.

Rick pressed his lips together. "I deserve her
censure, Mrs. Greenfield. But I'm going to try to
make things right. Miss Shaw, have you discussed
your plan with your parents?"

He hadn't expected to see such an expression of
guilt on the confident young woman's face.

"Mom, Will, I told him I wanted to keep Lindy here
with me. I know I should've asked you first but—"

"Of course, dear," her mother said. "She's such a little darling. We'll enjoy having her."

"Sure," Will agreed. "Actually, I figured you wouldn't want to let her go."

Rick frowned. "What do you mean? Why would you expect Vanessa—I mean Miss Shaw—to want to keep Lindy?"

Will smiled. "It's family history. Vivian and her first husband adopted Vanessa when she was a baby. After her father died, Vanessa learned from Vivian that she had five siblings in the world. Viv hired me to find them. I fell for her and convinced her to marry me. And we found all five siblings. One died in the war in Iraq. Vivian and Vanessa have tried to have all of them move in with us," Will added.

"And they didn't?"

"Several of them did for a short time. But they're all married now."

"So why would she want Lindy?"

"Because she needs me," Vanessa said firmly. "She's a lovely girl, but she hasn't been cared for and encouraged—she's been ignored. I had to go buy her some clothes just to get her home from the hospital."

"You mean you didn't pack up any of her clothes?"

"Didn't you see them in her closet?"

"Well, yes, but I presumed you'd picked out the best and packed them."

Vanessa shook her head. "No, I bought her a

couple of casual outfits to last her until I can take her shopping. And I ordered new uniforms for her school. She'd outgrown what she'd had for the past three years."

"I'll reimburse you at once," he muttered.

"And Betty, our housekeeper," Vivian began, "is in seventh heaven with a new person to cook for. She feels Lindy hasn't been properly fed." She paused. "Do you know if she's had regular visits to a doctor?"

"No, I don't." He held up a hand in Vanessa's direction. "I know, I know. I should have that information. As soon as I find another attorney willing to take on my personal business, I'll—"

"Do you have someone in mind?" Vivian asked.

"No. I had no idea that I'd be needing a new one."

"We can recommend Jeff Jacobs. His office is just a few blocks away," she replied.

Will added, "Jeff is Vanessa's brother-in-law. He's a fine lawyer."

"I need someone to give Miss Shaw temporary guardianship papers so she can take Lindy to the doctor or the hospital if necessary."

"Temporary? You'll leave her with me for at least a year, won't you?"

"I'll consider it, if the first few months go well."

Vivian said, "We have that in place for Danny."

Rick frowned. "Who is Danny?"

"He's our almost-three-year-old son. In case there was an emergency and Vanessa was notified before us—though we seldom leave him—she would be able to take Danny to the hospital."

"Did Jacobs handle that for you?"

"Yes, he did," Will said, nodding.

"Maybe I'll talk to him."

"Why don't you come to dinner tonight and we'll invite Rebecca and Jeff, so you can meet him."

"Mom, I don't think…" Vanessa began.

As if her negative reaction had pushed him into making a decision, Rick said, "Thank you. I accept."

"But what if Lindy—?" Vanessa protested.

"Surely as long as she knows I'm not taking her away from you, she can manage to be in the same room with me!" Rick said sharply.

"I think he's got a point, Vanessa. And I remember you saying she'd have to face her brother sometime." Will smiled at Vanessa.

"Yes, but I'm not sure she's ready."

"You'll have the afternoon to talk to her, dear," her mother said. "Betty will be thrilled to organize a dinner. I'm glad you've decided to join us, Mr. Austin."

"Make it Rick, please," he said.

"Of course, and call me Vivian."

"I think maybe we'd better all go to first names," Will added. "Seems we'll be seeing one another regularly for a while."

Before he replied, Rick turned to Vanessa. "Are you okay with that, Miss Shaw?"

She narrowed her hazel eyes. "If you insist… Mr. Austin."

VANESSA CREPT into Lindy's room, afraid the girl was still asleep. But Lindy was sitting at a window seat with Betty, who had stayed with her following the fainting episode. The housekeeper exited quietly.

When she saw Vanessa, Lindy seemed to shrink back.

"Do I have to go with him?" she asked in a quavery voice.

"No. He's agreed to let you stay here with me," Vanessa said with a warm smile.

Lindy bounded up as if Vanessa had pressed a button. "He did?" she asked incredulously. "Really?"

"Really, sweetheart."

"Oh, Vanessa, I'm so glad! I can't believe—"

"Wait, there's a catch. He's coming to dinner tonight."

A curtain fell over her smile, and panic rose in her eyes.

"It'll be okay, honey. He's not as bad as you said he was."

Lindy was unconvinced. "You're just saying that because he's handsome! That's what Mom always used to say."

"No, I hardly noticed his appearance." But she

couldn't lie to Lindy. Hadn't noticed? How could anyone help but notice his dark good looks? She revised her response. "Well, not much," she said honestly. "But he explained why he didn't come to see you."

"Because he didn't care about me."

"No. I'm afraid your mother was the reason." Under the circumstances Vanessa thought it best that Lindy know the truth. It might help the teen come to terms with her brother. "It seems she—she tried to seduce him after your dad's death."

While they hadn't talked much about her mother, Vanessa had realized Anita wasn't much of a parent. But she was all Lindy had had.

Lindy's eyes widened in surprise. Then she looked away. A moment later she turned back to Vanessa, sadness shadowing her face. "No wonder he avoided me."

Vanessa took her hand. "Lindy, he expected the lawyer to see you each month and determine how you were doing. The man was supposed to let him know if something was wrong."

Lindy stared at her, saying nothing.

"Obviously, your brother should've checked that the lawyer was doing his job properly, but Rick fired him today when he discovered the man had lied to him."

Lindy still said nothing.

"So, will you be all right with Rick coming to dinner?"

"Yes, of course. It's your house."

Vanessa paused. Then she asked, "Would you rather go back to the condo instead of staying here?"

"No!" was Lindy's sharp reply, reminding Vanessa a little of Rick Austin.

"Okay, then, let's go have some lunch, and later we'll go shopping!"

"What for?"

"New clothes for tonight. Your brother is going to pay for whatever you need."

"He doesn't mind?"

"No, honey. He thought your mother was buying you pretty clothes. Instead your mom spent all the money on herself."

Lindy's eyebrows rose. "He *wanted* me to have pretty clothes?"

"He did," Vanessa assured her. Tears filled her eyes at Lindy's look of awe, and she blinked to dam them. Forcing a smile, she pulled Lindy to her feet. "Come on, let's go eat."

LINDY WAS SO EXCITED, she didn't eat much lunch. She'd seldom been shopping, other than an occasional foray into Wal-Mart with an extremely limited budget. Today, Vanessa took her to the best store in Highland Park.

Because of Lindy's fair coloring, Vanessa steered

her toward a bright blue dress, modest but fashionable. "Try this one, Lindy. I think it'll look good with your blond hair."

The dress had cap sleeves and a heart-shaped neckline. The snug waist showed off Lindy's slight figure and made her look a little older than her fifteen years.

"Oh, I think that's perfect," Vanessa said. "What do you think?"

"It's beautiful." Lindy spoke softly, staring at herself in the mirror.

"Okay, try on this pink dress, and the black one, too, though I think you're too young for black."

"Should I wear black because my mother—"

"We don't want to be disrespectful to your mother, but frankly, she wasn't much of a mother."

"She wanted to look young so she could find a new husband," Lindy blurted out, suddenly sounding wise beyond her years. "That's why she didn't spend any money on me."

"Whatever her reasons, you should never have been treated that way." Vanessa smiled at her. "And I promise that will never happen again." They resumed their shopping, ultimately purchasing the blue and the pink dresses, not the black.

Then Vanessa took Lindy to her favorite salon for a trim and style.

"I—I've never been to a beauty shop," Lindy said nervously.

Vanessa's heart broke, but she hid her sadness. "I'll stay with you, honey. Don't worry, they'll make your hair look great. You'll see."

Vanessa also arranged for Lindy to have her nails done. The child was overwhelmed.

"Are you sure Rick will pay for this?"

"Yes, he will. You're still spending less than a quarter of the money your mother was spending every month. It'll be fine."

While the stylist was working on Lindy's hair, she told Vanessa about a sale at another store.

"We'll go there before we head home. I think you need some basics for your new wardrobe."

"We'd better wait and ask Rick, Vanessa. He might refuse to pay."

"He wouldn't dare," Vanessa said firmly.

"But he might think I was taking advantage—"

"Well, what do you think of your hair?" the stylist asked, interrupting their discussion.

Lindy looked in the mirror. Her blond hair was cut in layers, framing her face. "I think it looks great! I've never gotten it to look like that."

"It should be easy now. And your nails look lovely."

"Yes. I feel so—so elegant!"

"Good. That's the whole point," Vanessa said.

Once they were in the car, heading to the store the stylist had mentioned, Lindy balked. "But, Vanessa, I thought we would wait."

"No, sweetie, we're not going to wait. You've done without for too long."

By the time they finally arrived home, they were laden with packages.

"I think you'd better take a shower and rest for a few minutes," Vanessa told her. "I'll be up later to help you get ready."

"Oh, thank you, Vanessa. I'm so nervous about tonight!"

"You're going to look great."

Once Vanessa was alone, she removed the tags on Lindy's purchases and took all but the dress the girl was wearing that evening down to Betty to be quickly laundered. She also wrote a note and took it downstairs.

After leaving the laundry with Betty, she asked Betty's husband Peter, "Are you going to open the door for our guests tonight?" Usually Peter tended to the gardens and the cars.

"Sure will. Betty's fixing a grand meal, so she'll be busy."

"Then will you please give this note to Mr. Austin and ask that he read it before he joins us?"

"Which one is Mr. Austin?"

"He's the only one you won't know," she assured him.

Then she sprinted back up the stairs to get dressed herself. She'd bought a little makeup when Lindy wasn't watching. Later, Vanessa intended to instruct her on how to apply it. But first she showered and put on a black dress that was a little more sophisticated than Lindy's.

Her dark hair flowed around her shoulders, a perfect coiffure that she'd been wearing for a long time. Then she lightly did her makeup.

As soon as she was satisfied with her appearance, she went down to collect the laundry, now clean and folded, and brought it up to Lindy's room.

Lindy jumped up when Vanessa entered. "You look beautiful!"

"Thanks. You're going to look beautiful, too!"

"I don't think—"

"Come on. I'll show you."

Once Lindy was completely dressed, Vanessa applied some makeup to the girl's face. Then she turned Lindy to the mirror.

The girl stared at herself, reaching to touch the mirror. "Is this really me?" she asked softly.

In the flattering blue dress and slim heels, her hair and makeup lighting up her face, Lindy looked every bit the angel she was. Vanessa choked back her emotions. "Of course it is, honey. You got your mother's beauty…and your father's heart!"

"I hope so," Lindy said softly, almost as if saying a prayer.

RICK WASN'T SURE he should've agreed to dinner with Vanessa Shaw's family tonight. But he'd spent

the afternoon checking on Jeff Jacobs and his partner, Bill Wallace. They'd received high marks from
everyone Rick asked, so he wasn't worried about
meeting Jeff tonight.

He'd also made a few calls about Vanessa Shaw.
She checked out, too. And he was grateful to her, he
guessed. She was giving him a chance to redeem
himself. He'd messed up and betrayed his father's
trust by excluding Lindy from his life. She'd been an
adorable six-year-old, blond like her mother, and
he'd figured Anita would mold her in her own image.

Maybe he could have prevented that to some
extent, but it would have brought him into contact
with Anita. That thought made him feel sick to his
stomach. That was the reason he'd moved her and
Lindy out of the house. He'd inherited it, with no
stipulations. But he couldn't live there with Anita in
residence. So he'd bought her an exclusive condo and
doubled the money she was supposed to get.

And felt like he'd satisfied his conscience.

Until Vanessa Shaw had come along to point out
the holes in his plan. All of them affecting Lindy.

He was worried about meeting Lindy, all grown
up. He figured she hated him, and he didn't for a
moment think Vanessa Shaw would try very hard to
change Lindy's feelings about him. Vanessa herself
hadn't shown him any approval.

However, he didn't have much doubt about
Vanessa being good to Lindy. She was young to be

so protective of his sister, but maybe it was past time for someone to be kind to Lindy.

Still feeling guilty, he rang the doorbell at the Greenfield home, hoping the dinner would go smoothly.

An older man, one he hadn't met, opened the door.

Rick nodded to him. "I'm Rick Austin."

"Come in, Mr. Austin. I'm Peter, Betty's husband. Uh, I'm supposed to give you this and wait for you to read it."

Rick frowned as he took the note and read the flowing writing. Vanessa wanted him to know that his sister was wearing a new dress this evening and that he should compliment her on it.

He crumpled the note in his hand, leaving Peter watching him with a nervous expression.

"Thank you, Peter," Rick said, hoping to ease the man's apprehension. He resented the note because he *knew* how to behave. His own mother insisted on good manners. But maybe Miss Shaw—he corrected himself, Vanessa—had a point. He had seen his sister only once since she was six—today when she'd fainted at the sight of him. Maybe a pleasant compliment would enable things to proceed smoothly.

"Where am I to go, Peter?"

"This way, please." He turned and started down the hall, and Rick followed.

When Peter opened a door across from the library, Rick drew a deep breath. Then, pasting a smile on his face, he entered the room.

Vivian immediately rose to greet him. Once again he was struck by the petite woman's beauty. In her forties, she had strawberry blond hair with but a few strands of gray. She welcomed him and introduced him to Jeff Jacobs, his wife Rebecca, their children Joey and Jamie, as well as Jeff's partner, Bill Wallace, and his wife, Chelsea, who was obviously pregnant.

Will invited him to sit down, and Rick did so. But he didn't see Vanessa or Lindy.

Just as he was making conversation with the others, the door opened again. Vanessa, looking stunning in a chic black dress, entered the room, followed by a beautiful younger woman.

Rick stood and stared at the two women. He remembered the note he'd received. Of course, praise was due both for their appearance, but he couldn't help seeing his stepmother when he looked at Lindy. Her blond hair and slender figure looked so much like Anita's.

He crossed the room to greet them. "Hello, Vanessa. You look beautiful tonight."

"Thank you," she said coolly, and stepped aside for him to face his sister.

"You look very nice, Lindy. Like your mother," he couldn't help adding.

Lindy appeared stricken, and she let out a gasp.

Vanessa wrapped an arm around the child. "It's all right, Lindy. He didn't mean that."

"What do you mean?" Rick demanded. "She *does* look like her mother."

"The woman you hated? Does that mean you hate Lindy, too?"

"No, of course not— I mean— I don't know her!"

"Exactly. Let me assure you, she may look like her mother, but that's where the resemblance ends!" Vanessa exclaimed.

"Dear," Vivian said, "aren't you asking a little too much of Rick to react as if he knows his sister? He's scarcely seen her in nine years."

"And whose fault is that?" Vanessa demanded.

Jeff stood and joined Rick. "Maybe you should cut him some slack, Vanessa. He may have been careless, but he had no choice about leaving her with her mother, unless he knew of any abuse. Any court would agree with that."

Vanessa wasn't satisfied with legal obligations. "That still doesn't—"

At that moment Betty stepped into the room. "Dinner is served."

And that ended their conversation…for the time being.

Chapter Three

Vanessa had asked her mother to seat Lindy next to her, in case the girl continued to be nervous about her half brother. Vivian had done as Vanessa had asked, but she'd put Rick Austin across the table from Lindy.

However, much to Vanessa's surprise, Lindy seemed eager to talk to her brother.

"Rick, do you still live in Dad's house?" Lindy asked in a quiet moment.

He frowned. "Yes, of course."

"It's a wonderful house," Lindy said. "I remember thinking it was like a castle."

Rick gave her a surprised look. "A castle? It doesn't look anything like a castle."

Lindy withdrew immediately, and Vanessa intervened, telling Rick, "You'll have to remember she was only six years old. Is it here in Highland Park?"

"Yes, of course. I didn't think," Rick said, apologizing at once. "Would you like to visit the house?"

he asked Lindy. "I'll be out of town next week, but I'll let my housekeeper know you'd like to drop by, if you want."

"Is it still Mrs. Abby?" Lindy asked, but her enthusiasm seemed to have disappeared.

"Yes, it is."

Lindy turned to Vanessa. "She's a lot like Betty, Vanessa. You'll like her if you meet her."

"Of course, honey, I'm sure I will. Maybe your brother will tell us a convenient time. We wouldn't want to show up at an inappropriate moment." She sent a pointed look to Rick to let him know she'd understood his parameters…and didn't like them.

He squared his jaw but said nothing. Fortunately, Rebecca asked him a question that caused him to turn away.

Vanessa felt Lindy withdraw beside her, but she couldn't follow suit. She sensed that she had to be on alert whenever the man was near. He was dangerous, in so many ways. He was way too handsome. His good looks could make a susceptible woman believe anything he said. *She* wasn't susceptible, of course.

After they left the table, she whispered to Lindy, "Have you changed your mind about visiting the house?"

Lindy shrugged. "He doesn't want me there. I'll manage without seeing it." Her voice showed the hurt she was feeling.

When they settled for coffee in the morning room,

Vivian invited the children to join them, saying she seldom saw Rebecca's two anymore. After the children arrived, Vanessa noticed Lindy relax for the first time that evening, losing her self-consciousness with Jamie, Rebecca and Jeff's youngest.

A glance across the room told her she wasn't the only one who had noticed the change. Rick Austin had his eye on his sister, too. Good. She intended to have a word with Mr. Austin before he went home tonight!

Rick leaned close to Vivian and asked a question, then Rick, Jeff and Bill stood and left the room.

She asked, "Where are they going?"

Vivian said, "Rick asked if I minded if he talked to Bill and Jeff in private."

"Is he coming back in here?" Vanessa demanded.

Will said, "Why wouldn't he?"

Vanessa didn't say anything. Since her parents had supported Rick several times, she didn't want to tell them that she intended to chastise him in private. All the clothes she'd bought Lindy were worth nothing if her brother didn't show some acceptance. He was like an absentee father figure for Lindy. Vanessa didn't think it would be easy to make up for all the years of emotional neglect without some assistance from Rick.

She breathed a sigh of relief when the men returned half an hour later. All three looked pleased with themselves, so Vanessa guessed Rick had hired Jeff and his partner to handle his private affairs.

But he had better not think he could pass off Lindy to his lawyers. She wouldn't allow that. Besides, that plan had already failed.

Bill and Chelsea left first, Chelsea explaining apologetically that she had to go to bed early these days because of her pregnancy. Vivian immediately told her she had done the same. Rick stood to take his leave, too.

After a cautious glance at Lindy, Vanessa stood and moved to his side, asking for a private moment in the library.

"Why?" he asked.

"Because I would like to talk to you about your half sister."

"Look, I arranged with Jeff and Bill to handle everything. They'll give you the money for whatever you need to buy her. I don't think you'll be unhappy."

"This is not about the money!" she protested in a low voice. "Can we go to the library, please?"

"Fine!" He turned around, holding the door open for her.

After another quick look at Lindy, still playing with Jamie, Vanessa walked past him to the library across the hall.

She waited by the door until he entered and then shut it. "Please sit down." It was an order, even though she said *please*.

"Look, Vanessa, I've taken care of everything. If you'll talk to Jeff, you'll see."

"Jeff can't handle this problem."

"Why not?"

"Because he's not Lindy's big brother! For some reason, she craves approval from you."

"Fine. I approve of her. Will that do?"

"You just don't get it, do you. Your stepmother didn't only deprive Lindy of clothes and furniture. She deprived her of love. The child is an emotional wreck, and only someone in her family can make that go away. Since you're the only one she has, it has to be you!"

"What do you expect me to do? I don't even know her."

Vanessa drew a deep breath. She needed to stay calm and focused. "Why do you think your father made you Lindy's guardian if anything happened to her mother?"

Rick glowered at her.

Good, she thought. He needed to think about what he was doing.

"He didn't have anyone else to take care of her," Rick said, his voice low.

"That's what I would assume. Wouldn't he expect you to do what you could for her? To heal the hurts her mother inflicted?"

"*He* married her. Not me!"

The bitterness in his voice told Vanessa she still had some work to do.

"How about I make a suggestion, and we'll discuss whether or not you can handle it," she said softly.

"What?" he barked.

"Instead of telling Lindy she can go see the house when you're not going to be there, why not invite her to dinner and welcome her?"

"She said she wanted to see the house. I said she could."

"I didn't know Lindy's mother or her father. But I know which one she loved the most. Remember your emotions when your father died? Well, Lindy felt at least that bad. You were old enough to take care of yourself. She was left to a mean, hateful woman who gave her no love at all. Would it be so hard to let Lindy into your heart just a little bit?"

"Her mother—"

Vanessa put up a hand to stop him. "I know her mother was impossible. But Lindy's not. She's sweet and lovable. And she needs your approval. Please?"

"Fine! I can be home for dinner on Wednesday. I'll tell Mrs. Abby the two of you will be there."

"I don't have to come. You two—"

"No. You're the expert about all those emotions. You need to be there."

He'd trapped her, and there was no way out. "All right, I'll come. Wednesday night at seven?"

"Yes."

"You won't forget?"

"No, I won't. Now, if you have no objection, I'll be on my way."

"Wait! You need to invite Lindy yourself. And then tell her goodbye."

"Damn it! I told you you were invited!"

She stared at him.

"Fine!" He rose and headed for the door.

She'd won the round, so why wasn't she happy?

Because spending another night with Rick Austin was the last thing she wanted to do. For many reasons she thought it best to keep her distance from him— not least of which was the fact that the man was too attractive for his own good.

Or for hers.

RICK ENTERED THE OTHER ROOM, trying to put a smile on his face. It was what his father would've wanted, he told himself. He hated to think that he'd failed the man. He knew his father had loved Lindy, his cute, precocious little girl.

But now she was a child-woman and reminded Rick so much of her mother. A shiver ran through his body at the mere thought of Anita. He controlled himself and walked over to his sister where she played with Vanessa's niece.

"Lindy, I was thinking, if you don't mind waiting until Wednesday to come see the house, I'd be free that evening and you and Vanessa could come to dinner. Would that be all right?"

He watched Lindy's face light up like a spotlight and acknowledged to himself that Vanessa had been right. He hadn't been sure until then.

"Oh, Rick, that would be wonderful!" Her gaze

shifted to Vanessa, who'd come in behind Rick. "Wouldn't it, Vanessa? Can we go on Wednesday night?"

"Sure, Lindy. I'm free then if you are."

Lindy giggled, reminding Rick again that she was still maturing. "You know I'm free, Vanessa."

"Okay, then we'll plan on Wednesday night. What time, Rick? Will seven be okay?"

Rick turned around to glare at Vanessa while no one else could see him. She was playing him. They'd already agreed on the time. "Yes, seven will be fine."

"Then we'll look forward to seeing you Wednesday at seven."

He nodded and remembered to smile at Lindy one more time. Then he turned to Will and Vivian, who, it appeared, had been watching them all with interest. "I've got to go now. I enjoyed the evening and I'm very pleased with Jeff and Bill. Thanks for referring them to me."

Will stood and shook his hand and Vivian kissed his cheek. Her warm gesture surprised him.

"Come to dinner anytime you please, Rick. We always have plenty of food and we love the company."

He wouldn't take her up on it, but the offer was sweet. "Thank you, Vivian."

After he left the house, he got into his car to drive home. He had a lot to think about. And he couldn't help feeling a surge of anger toward Vanessa Shaw.

He'd forgotten she was studying to be a psychologist. She'd make a good one, he remarked to himself. She'd certainly found the right button to push and he'd done exactly what she wanted.

Normally he wasn't that easily manipulated. Dinner Wednesday evening wouldn't be exactly as she'd envisioned it.

He hit a button on his cell phone.

A silky voice answered. "Hello."

"Sharon, it's Rick."

"Oh, hi, lover. I missed you tonight."

He chuckled. That was her standard greeting, though he seldom saw her because of his travels. "Good. I'm having an intimate dinner party on Wednesday evening at seven. It will just be you, my sister and her guardian. Can you make it?"

"I didn't know you had a sister. But of course I'll be glad to come. I'm delighted to finally meet your family."

"Good. I'll see you then."

He shut off the cell phone, thinking about what she'd meant. When it hit him that Sharon thought he was getting serious about her, he almost stomped on the brakes. Damn! He'd let Vanessa get under his skin and trick him into doing the right thing. Then he'd tried to outsmart her, and now look at the mess he was in.

Sharon was a good date, presentable, sophisticated. She didn't require a lot of maintenance, either.

But he, unlike his father, did not intend to be caught by a pretty face or a good body. His stepmother had taught him that lesson.

Should he call Sharon back and cancel? No, he needed protection from Vanessa.

What was he thinking? He didn't need protection from any woman! He could handle himself... couldn't he?

THE EFFECT RICK'S INVITATION had on Lindy was remarkable. She always seemed to be smiling. And thinking about Wednesday. Monday, after a relaxing weekend, she announced, "It's only two days until Wednesday."

Vanessa looked up in surprise. "Well, yes, Wednesday is always two days after Monday, Lindy."

"Yes, but we don't always have an invitation to Rick's for dinner, you know."

"Ah, yes, I forgot about that." At Lindy's alarmed look, she hastily added, "Temporarily, of course. I have it written in my day planner."

"Oh, good. I was thinking maybe I could wear my new pink dress."

"That's a good idea."

"What will you wear?"

"Me? I don't think it matters what I wear. Rick will be focused on you, not me."

Lindy kept her head down, saying nothing for several minutes, but Vanessa waited patiently.

"Maybe…maybe Rick only invited me so you'd come," she finally said, almost in a whisper.

Vanessa put her arm around the young girl. "I can guarantee you that's not the case. Don't even give it another thought."

"Are you sure?"

"I'm sure. I think he realized he should be there the first time you come back to the family home. That's what his father would've wanted— Let me rephrase that. That's what *your* father would've wanted."

Tears filled Lindy's eyes. "I can't really remember him," she confessed. "When I think about him, I remember how he made me feel, rather than what he looked like."

"Don't you have a picture of him?" Vanessa asked, shocked.

"No. Mom didn't have any pictures of him. I asked her once, but she said no."

"Maybe while we're over there Rick will let you have a picture of your father."

"Do you think he might? I'd like that."

Vanessa made a mental note to call Rick later, when Lindy wasn't around.

Just then, the phone rang downstairs, which meant it was for her parents. Vanessa ignored it. Betty would answer it if her mother wasn't available. To her surprise, Betty called up the stairs for her.

"Excuse me, Lindy. I'll go see what Betty wants."

She quickly ran down the stairs to the kitchen.

"Vanessa. Your sister is on the line, wanting to know if Lindy could baby-sit tonight," Betty said. "She didn't want to call on your line because she figured Lindy would hear the conversation. She thought you should decide if you thought it was okay before she talked to Lindy."

"Oh. I'd better talk to her." She went to the phone in the library. "Becca? It's Vanessa. You need Lindy for tonight?"

"Yes. Jeff wants me to accompany him to dinner with one of his clients. We'll be home before ten. Do you think Lindy could baby-sit?"

"She probably could, but you could bring the kids over here."

"I know, but I thought it would be good for Lindy's self-esteem, and the kids will be in bed asleep when we get home, which will be nice."

"Okay. Do you want to talk to her?"

"I'll call on your line, if you want, and we can pretend this conversation never happened. Okay?"

"Sure. Give me a couple of minutes to get back upstairs. And, Becca? Thanks."

Vanessa could hear the smile in her sister's voice. When Rebecca said, "I wasn't around when you were little. It's the least I can do. And it helps me, too."

After hanging up, Vanessa hurried upstairs. Rebecca was right. Baby-sitting *would* help Lindy's self-esteem. She composed her features so Lindy wouldn't know what was happening until Rebecca called.

Lindy looked up. "Is everything okay?"

"Sure. Betty wanted to see if we'd be happy with what she was thinking about for dinner. But I told her we always love anything she fixes," Vanessa said with a smile.

Before Lindy could ask what was for dinner, which Vanessa realized would have been the snag in her story, the phone rang again. "Hello?" Vanessa answered. "Oh, hi, Becca. Yes, she's here." She handed the phone to Lindy, who looked apprehensive.

That apprehension turned to delight as Lindy listened to Rebecca's request. After agreeing to the offer, she hung up the phone and turned to Vanessa in excitement.

"She wants me to baby-sit! She said the kids like me and she thinks I'll be responsible! Isn't that amazing?"

"I think it's perfectly normal. How much is she paying you?"

"Paying me? Oh, no, she shouldn't pay me!"

"Why not?"

Lindy gave her a shocked look. "But I'm just— Isn't that something you do for each other?"

"Maybe, and she knows that I'd baby-sit for her, but she wants to have the kids in bed on time in their own beds. That means someone has to be inconvenienced by coming to her house. And *that* means she'll pay you."

"And you think I should accept it?"

"Yes, I think you should."

"I'll give the money to you, of course."

"Why would you do that?"

"To help pay for the things you've bought me."

Vanessa smiled and shook her head. "Your brother is paying for everything. You can offer him the money if you want, but he won't take it."

Lindy seemed thrilled, and wandered off to her room with a big smile.

Now that she was alone, it was time for Vanessa to put into action her earlier plan. Lindy wanted a picture of her father, and that's just what she would get. No matter that Vanessa had to go to Rick to get it.

Chapter Four

When Rick answered his cell phone after he got back to his hotel, a familiar voice sounded in his ear.

"Hi, Mrs. Abby. Everything okay?"

"Of course," his housekeeper replied. "But I have a question. Miss Shaw called earlier today. She asked if you had a spare picture of your father for Lindy. Apparently the child doesn't have a photo of him."

Rick couldn't think of anything to say. While he was annoyed that Vanessa had called, a sadness niggled at the thought that Lindy didn't have a picture of her own father. Every child should have that, he thought, and again he took responsibility for not thinking of that nine years ago. He'd just assumed Anita— He pulled up short on that thought; he should've known better than to expect anything from that woman.

Before he could reply, Mrs. Abby continued.

"Miss Shaw suggested I might find a photo or duplicate one so you could give it to Lindy Wednesday night. When I said I would, she said not to do it without checking with you first, because she didn't want to make you mad."

Rick growled inwardly. The sadness and sympathy he had felt for Lindy were pushed out by anger and indignation, thanks to that incendiary comment. To believe that—and to say it to his housekeeper! That was all he needed, for Vanessa to make him sound like an unfeeling animal.

"She sounded very nice on the phone," Mrs. Abby said. "Why would that make you mad?"

"It wouldn't have. She's a difficult female, that's all."

"Hmmm. Whatever you say. Well, I'll see you tomorrow night."

"Uh, Mrs. Abby," he said quickly, stopping her from hanging up. "How did Miss Shaw get my number at the house?"

"She said she'd spoken to your attorney." She paused. "That was all right, wasn't it?"

"Fine." No sense bringing his housekeeper into his feud with Vanessa. "I'll be home late tomorrow night. Don't wait up for me." He always said that, and she always did anyway.

"Yes, sir."

Rick shut off his cell phone before he let out a few choice words about Vanessa Shaw. She'd already disrupted his sleep since he'd met her. Now she'd managed to upset Mrs. Abby, too.

Of course he wouldn't mind giving Lindy a picture of their dad. He hadn't realized she didn't have one. Dad would've wanted— He wasn't going to think about what his dad would've wanted. Not now. That only led to thoughts about that damn Vanessa Shaw! And his own guilty conscience.

He was tired. Tonight he wanted to get a good night's sleep—at least one good night before he had to face Vanessa Shaw again.

VANESSA PICKED UP Lindy from her baby-sitting job when she called to say Rebecca and Jeff were home. Since they only lived five minutes away, it didn't take long. Lindy seemed happy, but when they got in the car, after saying goodbye, she almost exploded in excitement.

"Jeff paid me fifteen dollars, Vanessa! Fifteen dollars! I've never earned any money before. Can you believe he paid me that much?"

"Hmmm, I thought the going rate was maybe twenty dollars for the night," Vanessa said. "I didn't realize Jeff was cheap. I'll have to complain."

"Vanessa, no! You can't complain! I—"

Vanessa laughed. "I'm teasing you, honey. I think fifteen dollars is a generous payment."

"Oh! I can't believe you did that to me!" Lindy shouted before she began giggling. "You had me so worried."

"I'm glad you're not upset. And I'm glad you have a sense of humor. You've been too serious way too long."

"I know. But I didn't have anything to laugh about."

Vanessa reached out and caught Lindy's hand. "But your life has changed now, and you need to do a lot more laughing."

"Yes," Lindy agreed with a smile.

They rode in silence the rest of the way home. But when they were walking up the stairs on their way to bed, Lindy asked, "Do you think Rick laughs much?"

Vanessa didn't want to answer that question. But she believed in being honest if she could. So, after they reached the top of the stairs, she stopped and looked at Lindy. "No, honey, I don't. But I don't think that's any of my business."

"But, Vanessa, it's my business, isn't it?"

"I suppose so."

"And I'm your business, aren't I?"

"Yes, of course, honey, but—"

"So that makes Rick your business, too."

Vanessa turned and continued on to Lindy's room. Lindy followed her. When Vanessa got to the room, she sat down on the bed and patted the space beside her for Lindy.

"Sweetheart, don't you want to be my business?"

"Yes, of course."

"I'm glad. But Rick doesn't want to be part of my business. And if he doesn't want that, then there's nothing I can do for him."

"Maybe…maybe Wednesday night you could tell some jokes?" Lindy asked hopefully.

Vanessa chuckled. "Obviously you've never heard me tell a joke. I'm no good at that."

"Really? Do you know any jokes?"

"No, Lindy, I don't. If you laugh, maybe he'll catch on. Maybe just being around you will help him laugh more."

"But I don't think I'll see him much after Wednesday night. After all, he won't have the excuse of showing me the house."

"Perhaps you can invite him to dinner over here again later on. And I think we should invite Mrs. Abby to lunch before you start back to school. She'll want to see where you live, and meet Betty. That way, she'll know you're being well taken care of."

"I haven't seen her since I was six, when Dad was alive. Do you think she'll care?"

"Oh, I forgot to tell you. She called tonight to confirm Wednesday and she wanted me to tell you how much she is looking forward to seeing you."

"She did? You know, she and my mom didn't get along. I thought maybe she'd think I was like Mom, too." A worried look settled on her brow, and Vanessa couldn't help but put an arm around her.

"I don't think there's even a chance she'll think you're like your mom, honey. There's not a mean bone in you."

"Mom wasn't mean, Vanessa. I don't want you to think that. She just—just didn't think of anyone but herself. She told me it was because she grew up poor."

Vanessa didn't want to hear the woman's excuses. It didn't matter how she grew up. A child was a child, and she needed love and care from a parent who put her first, regardless of the mother's upbringing. But she'd spare Lindy another lecture tonight. Instead she said, "Well, Mrs. Abby will like you just the way you are, I promise."

Lindy smiled and nodded. "I'm so looking forward to Wednesday!"

"I know you are. But try to get some sleep between now and then or Mrs. Abby will think I'm working you to the bone!"

As Vanessa rose to leave, Lindy laughed. Vanessa bent to kiss the girl's cheek. "Good night, honey. I'll see you in the morning."

"Good night."

Vanessa went back downstairs. She wanted some decaf coffee before bed. She needed to think.

Betty was still in the kitchen when she entered.

"Why, hello, child. I thought you'd gone up already," Betty said.

"No, I thought I'd fix a cup of coffee."

"I'm fixing a pot now for your parents. They're in the library if you want to join them."

"All right, I will. Thank you, Betty."

She rapped on the door before she opened it. She didn't want to take her parents by surprise. Sometimes they acted like newlyweds.

"Mind if I join you?" she asked after she opened the door.

"Of course not, dear. Come on in," Vivian said. "What are you doing?"

"I was going to make myself a cup of coffee but Betty said to just come join you because she's bringing you coffee."

"We're glad you did," Will said. "Did you get Lindy home all right?"

"Yes. She was terribly excited, though. Jeff paid her fifteen dollars for baby-sitting."

Will smiled. "The first money you earn is always the biggest amount."

"Yes, and it occurred to me that I've never held down a job, except at school. So Lindy is ahead of me."

"So you're upset that I told you to study harder instead of taking a job away from someone who needed it?" Vivian asked.

"No, Mom, but—but I think I might've learned a lot by earning an honest paycheck."

"You want to fill in when Carrie goes on leave?" Will suddenly asked, leaning forward. His assistant, and Vanessa's friend, was having a baby. Vanessa would be an aunt again, since Carrie had married her brother Jim after helping to locate the missing sibling. Jim had just gotten discharged from the Marines, where he'd been a captain, and was now working at Will's private investigation firm.

"I'd love to help out, Will, but I have classes to teach."

"See? I think maybe your mother is pretty smart."

Vanessa laughed. "I get paid for teaching at the university. It's not much, but I do earn it. I meant when I was a teenager."

"Well," Will said, sitting back, "I can't help you there. I wasn't around then."

"No, Will, but I wish you had been. And I think Mom does, too." Vanessa looked at her mother for agreement.

"I'm not sure God would appreciate me agreeing with you, dear, but I can certainly say I'm glad he came along." She smiled lovingly at her husband.

He lifted her hand to his lips. "Me, too, sweetheart."

Vanessa smiled at the pair. She'd never seen her mother so happy as after she'd gotten together with Will. Not that her marriage to Herbert Shaw had been unlivable, but Will was warm, open about his feelings, demonstrative. They shared something really special.

Would Vanessa ever find that kind of happiness?

She'd dated some, had certainly had her share of boyfriends in high school and college. Lately, though, because she was involved with her doctorate and teaching, she hadn't had much time for romantic pursuits.

Did Rick have a girlfriend?

Where had that thought come from? Wherever it came from, she sent it back. There was no point in pursuing that line of thinking. Except for the fact that Rick Austin was Lindy's brother, the man didn't matter to her in any way.

Still, she asked her mother and Will, "What do you think about Rick Austin?"

Will's gaze sharpened. "Why?"

Vanessa didn't meet his eye. It was hard enough to admit to *herself* that she found the man interesting, much less to Will and Vivian. "I just wondered."

The two older people exchanged looks. Then Vivian said, "I like him. He seems to be a true gentleman."

"Of course he is to you, Mom," Vanessa said wryly.

Will sat up. "Are you saying he hasn't been a gentleman to you, Vanessa?" He was frowning.

"No, Will, don't go all protective on me. I'm just saying he—he doesn't treat me like he treats Mom."

"I don't blame him for that, Vanessa," Will said on a laugh.

Just then, Betty came into the library carrying a tray with coffee and cookies.

"Yum, Betty," Vanessa exclaimed.

"I brought cookies just because Mr. Will gets hungry late at night. But he might be willing to share."

"Maybe," Will said, but Vanessa saw him wink at Betty.

Betty smiled and left the room.

"Well, are you going to share, you rat?" Vanessa asked.

Vivian, reaching out for a cookie without asking,

said, "That's her favorite word. I've tried to persuade her not to use it, but I haven't had much success."

Will grinned. "Yes, the rat will share, child. Betty brought two for each of us."

"Ah, good." Vanessa got her coffee and two cookies and returned to her seat. Then she brought the conversation back to the man who occupied a lot of her thoughts. "Lindy is worried that Rick doesn't laugh much."

"What made her think of that?" Vivian asked.

"I was teasing her earlier and she started giggling. I told her I was glad she had a sense of humor, that it was important to laugh."

"That's true," Will agreed.

"So when we got home, she wanted to know if I thought Rick laughed much." She sighed before she said, "I had to be honest. I said no."

"He's a very serious young man," Vivian said.

"Yes, he is." So much so that it made her heart ache for him. She knew he felt guilty about Lindy, which was a good thing. In fact, she was relieved to know that he had a conscience. It made him appear different from her own father, thank goodness.

"What did Lindy say then?" Will asked.

"She wanted to know if I could tell some jokes Wednesday night at dinner."

Will burst out laughing, but Vivian sighed.

"She's such a darling, isn't she?" Vivian said.

"Yes, she is. Did you know she hasn't had a

picture of her father since he died? When I found out today I called his housekeeper and asked her to find one that Lindy could bring back home with her… after Mrs. Abby gets Rick's permission. I didn't want to appear to be doing something behind his back."

"Oh, I'm glad you did that, dear."

"Yeah," Will agreed. "Her mother has a lot to answer for, but I guess we'll have to leave that up to God, since she's already gone."

"Yes, I guess so." Vanessa stood. "Well, now that I've had my cookies and coffee, I'll go up to bed. I just wanted to—to get those things off my chest."

"We're glad you did, sweetheart. Sleep well."

Vanessa kissed both of them on their cheeks and headed for her bedroom. Will and her mom were always willing to listen. She didn't know what she'd do without them.

Not that she told them everything. Her true opinion about Rick Austin had to remain a secret. It would undermine her resistance to him if she ever let anyone know about that.

RICK HAD TOLD SHARON to be there at seven o'clock for dinner, but when the doorbell rang as the hall clock chimed the hour, he knew it wasn't Sharon. She was notorious for being late.

Sure enough, when he opened the door, his half sister and Vanessa stood there. "Come in. You're right on time."

"Vanessa said it would be rude to be late," Lindy said with a smile.

He wished Sharon showed that consideration. As he led them into the living room, he noticed Vanessa looking around, but he wasn't worried. His mother had bought the furniture and, in spite of his stepmother's protests, it had remained the same. To him, it was a warm, comfortable room.

He was startled to realize how perfectly Vanessa fit in the room.

Mrs. Abby, having heard the doorbell, followed them into the room and set down a tray of hors d'oeuvres. Her gaze flew immediately to the slim blonde sitting demurely on the sofa. "Oh, Miss Lindy, how you've grown!"

Lindy stood up. "I'm so glad to see you, Mrs. Abby," she said as she rushed into the woman's outstretched arms.

Mrs. Abby patted her hair and kissed her flushed cheek. "My, my, your daddy would be so proud of you now!"

Lindy's eyes filled with tears. "Would he?"

"Didn't Rick tell you that? Your daddy thought you were the most beautiful child. But you're even prettier now."

As if she were making a terrible confession, Lindy whispered, "Rick says I look like my mom."

"He's just fooled by the blond hair, that's all. Right, Rick?" Mrs. Abby challenged.

Rick recognized his cue. "Of course, as usual you're right, Mrs. Abby. May I introduce Vanessa Shaw?"

Mrs. Abby nodded. "I'm pleased to meet you, Miss Shaw. You must be taking good care of our baby for her to look so pretty."

"I can't take much credit for it, Mrs. Abby. Our housekeeper is trying to feed her all the time."

"Good for her. But it takes more than healthy food to make a girl happy. I bet you're responsible for that. Now, I'll go finish up dinner." After checking her watch and frowning at Rick she left the room.

He ignored her behavior. He knew she didn't care for Sharon, but he wasn't going to determine his dates based on Mrs. Abby's tastes.

He picked up a gift-wrapped package off the coffee table and handed it to Lindy. "Mrs. Abby got this for you."

Lindy eagerly unwrapped a framed picture of her father. "Oh, I *do* remember him! I wasn't sure."

"I'm glad you do. He loved you very much."

"He used to let me sit in his lap while he worked in the evenings. Then, when I got sleepy, he'd carry me up to bed and help me say my prayers. I can still smell his pipe smoke." Lindy's voice was dreamy, as if she'd traveled back in time.

"That's probably what killed him," Rick said.

Lindy let out a moan and Vanessa gasped. She wrapped an arm around Lindy. "How dare you say that to her!"

"What? What did I say?"

"Telling Lindy that she killed her father because he carried her up to bed! She couldn't have weighed much at all!"

"I didn't say that," he protested.

"Yes, you did!" Vanessa snapped back.

"I meant his *smoking*. He switched to a pipe, but he'd already smoked cigarettes far too long. That's what I meant."

Lindy relaxed against Vanessa's shoulder. "Oh, I thought you meant—" She sat up straight and forced out a smile. "He liked taking me up to bed, didn't he?"

"Of course he did," Rick replied. "If anything, that made him younger."

His words soothed Lindy. He wasn't sure Vanessa had forgiven him, though.

"Maybe we should go on in to dinner. My other guest seems to be late." He wanted to stop Vanessa from thinking about his gaffe.

They were crossing the hall to the dining room when the doorbell rang.

"Good. That will be Sharon." He opened the door.

Before he could greet Sharon, she slid her arm around his neck and pulled his head down for a long kiss. Then, when he pulled away, she said in a throaty voice, "Hello, sexy."

He pulled her arm down and turned her toward the other two guests. He hoped Vanessa wouldn't realize how embarrassed he was. "Sharon didn't know she had an audience. Sharon Cresswell, this is my baby sister, Lindy, and her companion, Vanessa Shaw."

The tall, curvy redhead came over and took Lindy's hand. "Well, aren't you the cutest little thing!"

Then she looked at Vanessa. "Hello, Vanessa. Long time no see."

"Hello, Sharon."

Rick frowned. "You two know each other?"

"We pledged the same sorority house," Sharon explained, "but Vanessa dropped out after one year."

"Dropped out of school?" Rick asked, surprised.

"No," Vanessa said coolly. "I just dropped out of the sorority."

"Uh, well, shall we go in to eat?" He reached out and took Lindy's hand as Sharon moved forward, expecting Rick to escort her into the dining room.

Rick led Lindy to the hostess's seat. "This is where you should sit, Lindy. After all, this is your home, too."

"I thought she was living with Vanessa," Sharon challenged.

"She is, but this is still her home," Rick said firmly.

Sharon pouted as she took one of the seats at the side of the table. Vanessa waited until Sharon had made her choice, then she moved to the other chair.

Almost at once, Mrs. Abby brought out the first course. After they were all served, Sharon leaned toward Rick and murmured to him that she'd seen a mutual friend that morning. While he acknowledged

what she'd said, he was well aware that she was
trying to exclude the other two guests. It struck him
that Sharon was using tricks as his stepmother had
done. He hadn't realized that before.

Watching Vanessa, he saw her lean toward Lindy
and say something. He couldn't hear the words, but
Lindy laughed, looking so happy.

He interrupted Sharon, saying loud enough for
the others to hear, "Sharon, Lindy was excited
because she earned money baby-sitting this week."

"Really? Well, Lindy, you should learn now that
that's not the way to get rich. What you do is find a
rich man and marry him. That's what I'm doing—
right, Rick?"

Rick froze. His other two guests looked embarrassed for him. "I wouldn't know, Sharon."

"Baby, don't be so shy. We can tell your sister,"
she assured him with a smile.

He frowned. "I still don't know what you're
talking about."

Sharon's face turned red. "So I'm fine to sleep
with, but not good enough to marry? I'll sue you for
all you're worth, Rick Austin!" She threw her napkin
on the table and stood. "Don't think you can sweet
talk me now, either. I refuse to listen."

Rick noticed that she was lingering, as if she
thought he would try to convince her to stay. He
stood. "I'm sorry you feel that way, Sharon. I'll walk
you to the door."

LINDY LEANED OVER to Vanessa, as they heard Sharon pleading with Rick, to ask, "Do you think he'll marry her?"

"I don't know, Lindy. It's obvious he didn't want to talk about it tonight."

"I hope he doesn't. If she only wants his money, why would he marry her?"

"Some men make inappropriate marriages because the woman is beautiful."

"You mean like my dad and mom?" Lindy asked in a small voice.

"I think your dad believed he'd be happy married to your mom. Otherwise, he probably wouldn't have married her."

"Yes, but I stayed at home with Daddy. She didn't."

"The marriages in my family aren't like that. The couples do most things together."

"I think I'd like a marriage like Will and Vivian's," Lindy said slowly. "They seem to like each other a lot."

Vanessa smiled. "I think that's important."

Rick suddenly came back into the room to rejoin them, looking flushed. "I apologize for Sharon."

"That's all right," Vanessa said. "People have arguments all the time."

"She said she was jealous of you," Rick announced, staring at Vanessa.

"I beg your pardon? Why would she be jealous of me? I wasn't flirting with you."

"Probably because you're prettier than her," Lindy pointed out.

Vanessa turned a frown on Lindy. "Sharon is a very attractive woman."

"But—" Lindy began.

Vanessa simply said, "Lindy."

"Yes, ma'am."

"I don't think you have the right to stifle my sister in her own house, Vanessa," Rick said.

"If she's in my care, then I'm responsible for her behavior." To defuse the volatile exchange, Vanessa changed the subject. "Lindy, did you tell your brother we have to go to the school and choose what you intend to study this year?"

"When do you do that, Lindy?"

"Next week. We have to call tomorrow to make our appointment."

"Should I go with you, too? To help you decide what you want to study?" Rick asked his half sister.

Lindy brightened. "Would you do that?"

Vanessa went on alert. There was really no need for him to get involved; she had it under control. "I don't think—"

But Lindy spoke up, cutting her off. "I'd really like that, Rick."

"What are your choices?" he asked, ignoring Vanessa as if she hadn't voiced an objection. Or tried to.

"I have a book with them listed," Lindy said. "I

can't remember all of them. Maybe you could come to dinner on Sunday and we could look at them together. Would that be all right, Vanessa?"

Now they noticed her, she thought, just when they could put her on the spot. She couldn't very well say no now. "Of course, Lindy," she said reluctantly.

Rick smiled broadly at Lindy, then Vanessa. "What time should I come?"

"We usually dine at one, after everyone gets out of church," she said. Then, giving it one more try, she said, "But if that's not convenient—"

Rick put up his hand. "I'll make sure it is. After all, it's what our dad would have wanted."

Vanessa glared at his pompous face. He knew he'd won this round. There was no way she could possibly decline him now, not when he'd used her own words against her.

No, she was stuck with him another day.

Chapter Five

"Are you mad at me?" Lindy asked anxiously after they started the drive home.

"No, of course not. I just have a lot to think about," Vanessa said.

"Rick said he'd help me pick my classes. I didn't think he'd ever want to see me again. Isn't that cool?"

"Yes."

"You don't mind, do you? I mean, I know you were going to help me, but Rick said he would and—"

"Yes, Lindy, I heard. That's fine."

"Okay," Lindy said, staring straight ahead.

Vanessa pulled the car into the driveway and turned off the motor, but she didn't open her door. "I'm very pleased that your brother is showing an interest in you. But I want you to remember that the choice is yours. He's an important man and is responsible for a large corporation. That tends to make him autocratic. I just want you to choose what is right for you, not what is right for him."

"I will, Vanessa, I promise. Besides, you'll be with me, too, won't you?"

"Yes, I will," Vanessa said. She didn't intend to let Lindy's brother run her over, as her own father had tried to do to her. She got out of the car, hoping she'd made her point. The change in Rick Austin tonight had been dramatic. Lindy was clutching the picture of her father and feeling restored to the family. All that was good. But how long Rick's attention would remain on Lindy, Vanessa wasn't sure. And his reason for changing bothered her, too.

She hoped she was wrong in thinking he'd changed to get back at her.

She was sure he'd invited the redhead just to irritate her. That was obvious when he shuffled Sharon out the door after she didn't behave as he wanted. Vanessa shook her head. If he married Sharon, he'd receive the same treatment his father had in his marriage. It would be a disaster.

Especially for Lindy.

The child would disintegrate in a battle with Sharon, a woman who wouldn't hesitate to play dirty. Vanessa had known Sharon well years ago when they were sisters in the sorority.

She followed Lindy upstairs. The child seemed to have forgotten about Sharon and the demonstration of intimacy between her and Rick. Maybe he'd broken it off with the woman tonight, but Vanessa didn't think Sharon would disappear that easily.

"Lindy, if Sharon contacts you for any reason, don't agree to anything until you check with me. Promise?"

"Why?"

"Because she'll try anything to get what she wants. No matter who it hurts."

"But Rick told her to leave."

"I know he did, but that doesn't mean she's out of his life. Just remember not to agree to anything, okay?"

"Sure, Vanessa."

After Lindy had gone to sleep, Vanessa made another trip down to the kitchen. There she gave Betty and Peter the same warning about Sharon.

"Sharon?" Betty asked. "The only Sharon I know is that awful girl in your sorority."

Vanessa nodded. "That's her."

"Why would she want to talk to Lindy?"

"She's been dating Rick, apparently. He sent her home tonight, but she won't chance losing someone rich like Rick that easily."

"Oh, you're right. She used to say years ago how she was looking for a rich man. And Rick is rich, isn't he?"

"Yes. He could end up unhappily married just like his father. That would be sad."

"Can you save him?"

"He's not my business. I'm just trying to protect Lindy." The truth was, however, she wanted to save him. It had appalled her when she'd discovered he was dating Sharon. She'd been having kinder thoughts about Rick lately, and Sharon had knocked all those out of her head. She couldn't believe the man could be so stupid!

After leaving the kitchen, she headed to the library, where she knew she'd find her parents. But only Will was there.

"Where's Mom?"

"She was tired, so I told her to go on to bed. I'm about ready to join her."

"Oh. I thought— Never mind." She and Will walked up the stairs together. "You don't think Mom is coming down with something, do you?"

"No, but if she's not better in the morning, I'll take off work and get her to a doctor."

"Good. I have an early meeting in the morning with Dr. Cavanaugh, but I'll check on her when I get back home."

They exchanged good-nights and she went to bed, but she couldn't keep her mind off Rick Austin…and Sharon. And it bothered her that everyone kept asking her what she was going to do about it. Rick wasn't her responsibility. The last thing she wanted to think about all night was Rick Austin.

When her alarm went off in the morning, she had to drag herself out of bed. She couldn't miss the meeting. It would determine her schedule for the upcoming school year. She was hoping to schedule all her classes while Lindy was in school. Then she could pick Lindy up when her classes let out.

Of course, Peter could get her, Vanessa thought. But she'd always liked it when her mother picked her up. She hoped to do the same for Lindy.

Betty stepped out of the kitchen when she heard Vanessa's steps on the stairs. "You can't go out without breakfast. I'll whip up something real quick."

"I can't, Betty. But I'll take a diet cola."

Betty fetched her a cola and a blueberry muffin. "Eat this on the way. That way you'll have something in your stomach."

Vanessa smiled. "Thanks. And remember, no Sharon."

"I'll remember."

The meeting took over an hour and a half. Vanessa was sure that by the time she got home Lindy would be up and in the kitchen with Betty and Peter, and maybe her mother. She hoped her mother wasn't coming down with something. But with Danny going to play-dates, he was probably being exposed to all sorts of germs, which meant her mother was, too.

She pulled into the drive and parked her car. When she came in the back door, she noticed Peter going to the front door. He opened it to the one person she didn't want see coming to call.

Sharon.

"I'll take this, Peter. Thank you," said Vanessa.

With a relieved expression, Peter went back into the kitchen.

Vanessa took his place in the doorway, one hand holding the door, the other braced against the jamb. "Hello, Sharon. What can I do for you?"

"I thought I'd visit with Lindy."

"I'm afraid she's busy."

"How do you know if you just came in?"

"Trust me, I know."

"Well, I'd like to take her shopping. When would be a good time?"

"I'm sorry, but I take her shopping often. She doesn't need any other trips."

"What's with you, Vanessa? Don't trust me with the little sister?"

"No, I don't."

"You're being silly. I just want to become friends with Lindy. After all, when I marry Rick, I'll be her sister-in-law."

"Perhaps you will, but that doesn't mean you can take her out now."

Sharon put her manicured hands on her hips. "You bitch! You're just hoping to keep Rick for yourself. But I've already got him, and you don't have a chance!"

Maintaining her composure, Vanessa replied calmly, "That's between you and Rick. But Lindy is my business and I'm keeping her here."

"We'll see about that. I'm telling Rick. He'll take Lindy away from you!"

Vanessa just stood there staring at her. Finally, Sharon stomped down the sidewalk. Vanessa watched her until she pulled her vehicle away from the curb.

She went into the kitchen where her mother and Lindy sat at the big round table with Peter and Betty. Peter jumped up and held out a chair for her. Betty immediately began cooking pancakes for Vanessa.

"Betty, I shouldn't— Okay, just one stack. I love your pancakes."

Peter poured her some coffee and brought it to her.

"You two are wonderful at spoiling me," Vanessa said with a satisfied sigh. She looked at her mother. "Are you feeling all right this morning?"

"Yes, I'm fine. Lindy and I had a contest to see who could eat the most pancakes."

Lindy grinned. "I won!"

"Good for you, I think."

"How did your meeting go, dear?" Vivian asked.

"Fine. I'm teaching nine hours, all of them on Monday, Wednesday and Friday ending at noon. It's a wonderful schedule."

"Three classes in a row? Won't that be tiring?" Vivian asked.

"Not really. Two of them are intro classes and the one at eleven is a class for kids who think they want to major in psychology."

"That sounds interesting," Lindy said. "Will they have psychology classes for me to take in high school?"

"I'm not sure, but we can look in the book you

have listing the classes. We'll do that after I eat my breakfast."

"Okay. Oh, look, here's Danny," Lindy said as the sleepy little boy wandered into the kitchen.

"Oh, my, Danny," Vivian said, holding out her arms. "I intended to come up to wake you, but I got busy talking and didn't realize how late it is. Would you like Betty to make you some pancakes?"

Betty was already at the stove, fixing silver dollars for the boy while Peter poured some milk for him.

Danny leaned back against his mother's shoulder. "I'm very hungry, Mommy."

"I bet you are. You didn't eat much dinner last night."

"Did he not feel well, either?"

"He was feeling perfectly well. As was I. You know how Will worries if anything is different. I was just a little tired."

"Are you sure you don't want any coffee?" Betty asked. "It might help you wake up."

Vanessa turned to stare at her mother. "You didn't drink any coffee?"

"No, I wanted milk to go with the pancakes."

Vanessa realized the only time she'd seen her mother turn down coffee was when she was pregnant with Danny. "Mom, you aren't!"

Her mother looked away. "I don't know what you're talking about."

"Lindy, will you keep an eye on Danny and help him put syrup on his pancakes?" Vanessa asked.

Lindy agreed. Vanessa got up. "Betty, you need to come with Mom and me."

Betty was frowning deeply as she followed Vanessa and Vivian into the library. "Now, Vanessa, what's the matter?"

"Betty, when was the last time Mom gave up coffee?"

Betty appeared to be studying the question, and then the answer dawned on her. "No! Are you? Miss Vivian, are you pregnant again?"

At first Vivian kept her head down. Finally, she raised it and said, "I think so."

"But I thought Will said no more babies," Vanessa said.

"I know. But I forgot to buy more birth control pills. I only missed two days, and I thought—"

"Oh, Mom," Vanessa said. "You've got to get to the doctor at once, to be sure that everything is all right. Why don't I take you now? Then you can tell Will tonight."

"I'm almost afraid to," Vivian said.

"Mom, you know Will. He loves you and Danny."

"But I don't think I can tell him."

"Let's get you to the doctor first. Then we'll worry about telling Will."

"Vanessa, you're such a good girl."

"That she is, Miss Vivian," Betty said. "I don't see how Mr. Will could resist another little one. You have nothing to worry about."

Vanessa shared a smile with Betty. "I think she's right about that. Are you ready to go?"

"Yes, but we should call first."

"I'll do that. Go get your purse," Vanessa said. She picked up the phone and dialed her mother's doctor, who was also hers, and asked for an appointment. When she explained the reason for the appointment, the nurse checked with the doctor, then came back to the phone and told Vanessa to bring her mother and they would work her in.

Once they reached the doctor's office, it didn't take long for them to call Vivian. She was clutching her daughter's hand, so Vanessa went in with her.

After a brief examination, the doctor looked at the two of them. "You are correct, Vivian. You're about six weeks pregnant."

"Is everything okay?" Vivian asked, her voice shaky.

"So far, so good. You remember all the rules?"

"Yes. Eat well, but not too much, no caffeine, and rest a lot."

"Good. At your age, you know you're a high-risk pregnancy. So I want to see you every two weeks. When you get to around seven months, I'll see you every week. Probably there won't be a problem since this is your second pregnancy, but we want to stay on top of things."

"Yes, of course."

"I assume Will is excited," the doctor said as he turned away to write on his chart.

Vanessa put her arms around her mother as Vivian's eyes filled with tears.

He glanced over his shoulder and spun around. "Vivian? What's wrong?"

"He doesn't know, Doctor," Vanessa said. "Mom is a little worried because he told her no more babies. He was afraid she might have difficulties."

"You are going to tell him now, though." It was a statement.

"Yes, of course," Vivian exclaimed with tears in her voice.

"If he has any questions, tell him to call me."

Vivian nodded as Vanessa helped her down from the examination table.

Once they were outside the doctor's office, Vanessa said, "Do you want to go tell Will now?"

"No. I'm rather tired. I think I should take a nap. Maybe—maybe I can tell him tonight."

Vanessa didn't think her mother sounded too sure of that, but she didn't say anything.

Once they got home, she helped her mother get to bed. Then she asked Betty to take some lunch up before Vivian went to sleep.

She found Lindy and Danny in the morning room. The little boy was playing with his trains while Lindy was doing her summer reading for school.

Lindy looked up as she entered the room. "How's Vivian?"

"She's fine. Just a little run down." After reassuring her, Vanessa asked, "Have you heard from your brother today?"

"No. Should I have?"

"No. Everything's fine," she lied. How could she tell the girl she expected Rick to blast her for throwing his girlfriend off her front step this morning? "Well, I've got an errand to run. I should be back before Danny gets up from his nap. I appreciate you taking care of him this morning."

"He's such a good little boy—aren't you, Danny."

"I'm a *big* boy." He stood on his tiptoes, stretching as high as he could.

"Of course you are, little brother." Vanessa hugged him to her. "I love you."

"I love you, too, 'Nessa. And Lindy, too."

Lindy beamed at the boy. "Thank you, Danny. I love you, too."

"Goodness, we've got lots of sugar in here. Maybe you shouldn't have any dessert after lunch."

Danny protested at once, and Vanessa told him she guessed he could have one cookie.

They heard the phone ring in the other room and Vanessa started to go answer it, but Peter appeared before she reached the door.

"Vanessa, the phone call is for you."

"Thank you, Peter." She went to the library to take it.

"Hello?"

"Vanessa, did you talk to Sharon today?"

Just as she'd expected. Rick Austin. And he was as mad as a bull.

She adopted a civilized tone and said, "Hello, Rick. Yes, I did."

"Why were you so mean to her?"

Vanessa sat down. "How was I mean to her?"

"You're keeping Lindy from her, and she's just trying to be kind."

"I don't consider her to be an appropriate companion for Lindy."

"Why?"

"She wants to be friends with Lindy so she can marry you. When or if you marry her, she won't want to spend any more time with Lindy, because she will have achieved her goal."

"You don't know that."

"Do you want to risk Lindy's happiness on that answer?"

"You're just being overprotective."

"Considering that no one cared for your sister for nine years, being a little overprotective doesn't seem like such a bad idea."

"So what if I marry Sharon?"

Vanessa had to clamp down on the horrors that question brought to mind, echoes of his father's second marriage. "Then you'll be presenting Lindy with the same kind of woman her mother was. And I think she should be protected from that."

"Sharon isn't that bad."

"I heard her say she was marrying you for your money." The man was supposed to be a brilliant businessman and he couldn't see what kind of woman Sharon was? What was wrong with him?

"She says that, but I don't think she means it."

"Well, when you marry her, I'll make sure I keep Lindy from having anything to do with her. Count on it!" She hung up the phone. She grabbed her purse and keys and stuck her head in the kitchen, telling Betty, "I'm going out."

She heard the phone ringing, but she ignored it. After all, she knew who was calling.

When she reached the office of Will's investigative firm, she hurried up the stairs. Normally, she wouldn't interfere in any problem her parents were having, but her mother seemed really nervous about Will's reaction.

Vanessa didn't think he would be too upset as long as he knew her mother was healthy. So she was going to break the news to him, in the hope that he could reassure her mother at once.

"Hi, Vanessa," Carrie called out, maneuvering her large pregnant belly around a file cabinet.

"How are you doing?"

"Fine. I just don't move as quickly as I used to." Carrie patted her belly and smiled.

"But the baby's due in a couple of weeks, right?"

"Yes, thank goodness. Are you here to see Will?"

"If he's available."

"Sure. Will? Vanessa is here to see you," Carrie called.

Vanessa walked into Will's office and closed the door behind her.

"Well, hello, Vanessa. Are we sharing secrets?" he asked, nodding toward the closed door.

"Yes, we are."

Anxiety instantly crawled into his voice. "What is it? Is something wrong?"

"Stay calm, Will. I took Mom to the doctor's office this morning. Everything's fine, but Mom is about to have a nervous breakdown about what the doctor told her."

"Why would she do that if everything is fine?" Will asked.

"Because you told her no more babies."

Will stared at her. "You—you mean she's pregnant?"

Chapter Six

Vanessa sighed. For the second time that day she was having to deal with a man who didn't seem to understand his woman. "Yes, of course that's what I mean."

Will just stared at her.

"Perhaps you don't remember telling her no more babies, but she does. She's in an emotional state that I don't think is good for her right now. You need to come home and reassure her…if you can."

"I was just worried about her health," Will assured her. "Having another baby at her age."

"So you'll be happy and supportive when you come home?"

"Of course. But she was on birth control pills. How—?"

"Will, she'll probably explain, but if she doesn't, don't ask. At least not today."

Will stood. "Then I'd better get home to Vivian." He looked at Vanessa again. "Are you okay? Has something else upset you?"

She let out a big sigh. "Men can be so dumb sometimes."

"Are you referring to me?" He sounded sheepish.

"No, not really." Because now wasn't the time for the conversation, she shrugged it off. "Go on home to Mom. I'll stay and talk to Carrie for a little while."

"Good. I don't really want to leave her alone, and Jim and Alex aren't due back for a while." He gave Vanessa a hug and hurried out of the office.

Vanessa returned to the outer office.

Carrie immediately asked, "What's wrong?"

"It's just men. They can be so—so difficult!"

"Are you talking about Will? I thought he was pretty far developed," Carrie said with a grin. When Vanessa didn't laugh, Carrie studied her friend. "Is anything else bothering you?"

"Why does everyone ask me that?" Vanessa said. She was beginning to think she had Rick Austin's name pasted on her forehead!

"You just seem a little off key, I guess."

"I had a difficult time with Rick Austin. He is so stupid!"

"Really? Will was quite impressed with him."

"Do you remember Sharon Cresswell from college?"

"The slinky redhead who was constantly on the hunt?"

"That's her. That's who Rick is dating. And she's trying to get to him through Lindy."

"Oh no! And you're right. If Sharon has fooled him, he must be really dumb. She's got dollar signs in her eyes."

"Exactly. And I won't have her using Lindy to get to Rick. As soon as she marries him, she'll ignore Lindy, just like her mother did."

"Poor Lindy. A double blow might just be too much."

"Yes. So I told him Lindy would have nothing to do with Sharon."

"Good for you. What did he say about that?"

"I don't know. I hung up and left the house."

"He'll be furious when he catches up with you."

Vanessa sighed again. "I know. That's why I'm not anxious to go home. Have you had lunch?"

RICK KNOCKED ON THE FRONT DOOR, determined to have it out with Vanessa. She had no business interfering with his private life, and he intended to tell her that in person.

Peter answered the door. "Hello, Mr. Austin. Please come in."

"Thank you, Peter. I need to speak with Vanessa."

"She isn't here right now. Mr. Will is home. Would you like to talk to him? He's in the library."

He entered and followed Peter. "When do you expect Vanessa?"

"I don't know, sir. She just said she was going out."

"I see."

When they reached the library, Peter asked, "Would you like some coffee? I'll bring in a tray at once."

"That would be nice, thanks." Peter returned to the kitchen while Rick stopped at the threshold. "Will? Am I disturbing you?"

Will looked up from where he sat on the sofa. "No, not at all. Come on in. What are you doing here in the middle of the day?"

"I had hoped to find Vanessa here." He walked in and stood by the fireplace.

"I think she's at the office with Carrie. I don't like to leave Carrie alone right now."

Since Rick looked confused, Will added, "She's pregnant and due in about two weeks, but babies are unpredictable."

"Oh. She's your secretary?"

"She was, but now she's an investigator, like her husband, Jim, and Alex, David's wife. I don't think you've met either of them, but Jim and David are Vanessa's brothers."

"I see." He was seeing that the family was very close. "Do you think Vanessa will be back soon?"

"Probably not for an hour or two. Be glad. She tore into me a little while ago, so it'll be better if she has time to cool off."

"I think that must've been after she chewed on me. She actually had the nerve to hang up on me."

"What did you do?"

"A friend called and wanted to take Lindy shopping, trying to be nice. Vanessa dismissed her rudely. I want to know why."

"Is this friend someone you can trust?"

Rick's head snapped up. "What do you mean?"

"I mean that sometimes a woman will lie, especially about another woman's treatment of her. Can you trust her judgment?"

Rick stared at Will as he sifted through his history with Sharon. He had to be honest. "Maybe not."

"You might've taken a different approach if you'd thought about that fact."

"You're right. But I took her at her word. It didn't occur to me that she would lie about something so— so inconsequential."

"Why did she want to take Lindy shopping?"

"To be nice to her. At least, that's what she said."

"And what did Vanessa say?"

"She said Sharon is just like my father's second wife."

Will raised his eyebrows. "And you're dating her?"

Rick shrugged. "I've taken her out occasionally. Usually when I need a companion for the evening."

"So now she thinks you're going to marry her?"

"No, of course not!" He tempered his outburst with, "At least, I don't think so."

"Then why is she trying to get close to Lindy? Because she loves children?"

"No. She has no patience with children," Rick said slowly, Will's point hitting home. He sent him an apologetic look. "I guess I should've been more suspicious of her before now. I just took her at her word."

Will chuckled. "Even good women don't come straight out with what they're doing or how they feel. It's too risky. But a mean woman is sure to spin circles around you until you can't think at all, like a spider spinning her web. That's when she's got you."

Rick had visions of a deadly black widow. "That's not a pleasant thought."

Will nodded. "It pays to be on your guard."

Rick stood there, thinking about facing Vanessa now. His contemplations were interrupted by Peter, who entered holding a tray with coffee and brownies.

"Thank you, Peter," Will said. He turned to Rick. "Come sit down, Rick. We'll discuss the world's problems while we have some sugar. Betty's brownies are wonderful."

Rick moved to sit beside Will. "I think instead of discussing the world's problems, I'd like you to tell me about Vanessa."

Will poured the coffee, then sat back with his. "I don't know what to tell you. Except that I trust her. Her judgment is good. She's usually honest, and she has good intentions. She understands people. She always completes whatever she has assigned to her. Like Lindy. She'll fight to the death for what she believes is right."

Rick sighed. "She sounds like a saint." A very beautiful saint.

:"Nope," Will said with a grin. "She's not a saint. She can make mistakes, but she tries to correct them if she does. She's very loving, warm-hearted."

"So if I tell her I've given up Sharon, will she take her place?"

Will stared at Rick. "What are you talking about?"

"Oh, I should explain. Occasionally, I need a companion for the evening, to even out the numbers, keep the conversation going, that sort of thing. And to look stylish and pretty. I used Sharon for that, and she was happy to be used. But if I'm not going to take Sharon, I need to find someone else to take her place. Do you think Vanessa will go with me?"

"I sure wouldn't ask her that way," Will said. "No woman wants to be used."

"I see what you mean, but—" Rick was confused. He was the CEO of a major international corporation; he'd never had difficulty communicating. Why was he having trouble now?

Vanessa did this to him. She made him think differently—about Lindy, about his father, about himself. And he wasn't accustomed to someone challenging him, second-guessing his decisions like she did.

Will must have read his confusion, because he explained, "Why not say it like this— 'Vanessa, you're right. I have to get away from Sharon. She's not good for Lindy, like you are. But I used Sharon to have a date for social occasions that I couldn't get out of. Is it possible you'd help me out on an emergency basis until I find someone else?' You see where I'm going with this?"

He did. He also thought Will Greenfield was pretty savvy. "I think I should've written that down, but I got the gist of it. Thanks for talking to me, Will. I know you're not as old as my dad would be if he were alive, but I miss having someone older to talk to."

"Glad I could be of some help. Someday, maybe Danny will be looking for some help because I'm not around. Maybe he can come to you." Will clapped him on the shoulder.

"I'm not sure I'll be as wise as you, but I'd be willing to listen to him. After all, he'll be raised as an only child like I was for sixteen years."

"You forget, he has Vanessa." Will stared down into his coffee. "And in seven and a half months he'll have another sibling."

Rick stared at Will. "Are you saying— No, you can't mean— Are you expecting another child?"

Will looked up. "Yeah. That's why Vanessa was mad at me. She's very protective of her mother."

Rick listened as Will related the morning's confrontation. Will was grinning by the time he finished.

"You didn't mind her telling you about the baby?"

"No, not at all. Vivian was really upset and that's not good for the baby. Besides, I'm thrilled now that the doctor says all is well."

"Then, congratulations." He shook Will's hand.

"Thanks, Rick."

They both heard the back door open and close. Will looked at Rick. "Are you ready?"

Rick nodded, but his pulse was racing at the thought of facing Vanessa.

Will stepped into the hall. "Vanessa? Is everything all right at the office?"

"Yes, Will," she called. "Did you talk to Mom?"

"Yes. She's sleeping peacefully now. Danny's down for his nap, too, and Lindy is reading in her room."

Vanessa sighed. "Oh, good. I'll—"

"You have a visitor here in the library," Will said. "Since you're here, I'll go check on your mother."

He moved out of the library and Rick waited for Vanessa to make an appearance. When she came to the door, Vanessa didn't look happy to see him. He stood and invited her to join him for the last of the brownies.

"I'm surprised there are any left. Weren't you and Will hungry?"

"Just me. I haven't had lunch. I came to see you first."

Vanessa, instead of sitting down, said, "Just a minute," and left.

Rick stared after her, not sure she would return. But she reentered the library a minute later. "Betty is fixing you a sandwich."

Rick frowned. "I don't need her to do that. I've gone without lunch before."

"I'm sure you have, but Betty doesn't believe in skipping meals."

"But it's not her job to feed me."

"No, but you don't seem to be doing a good job of it." As if dismissing the discussion she waved her hand, then sat opposite him. "Will said you wanted to see me?"

"Uh, yeah. I've been thinking, and I think you're right."

Vanessa, who had opened her mouth to speak, abruptly shut it. "What did you say?"

"Something I didn't expect to say. But Will helped me figure out what was wrong with the picture I was seeing."

"He did?"

"Yeah, he asked me if I could trust Sharon. I realized immediately I couldn't. So you're right. I don't want her to be around Lindy. *I* don't want to be around her."

"So we don't have a problem?"

"Well, yes, we do, but—"

Betty came through the door with a sandwich and chips for Rick. "You should've spoken up when you got here, young man. I love to feed a hungry man." She beamed.

"Thank you, Betty, but I didn't want to cause any trouble."

"No trouble at all. And you eat every bit of it. You're a big man. You need to eat regularly."

After Betty left, Rick said, "I feel like the bull in the china shop."

"She didn't mean it that way. But she thinks a man can't miss a meal or he'll faint dead away."

"Well, she may have a point after all. I'm feeling a little faint right now."

Vanessa gave him time to eat some of his lunch. But finally, she could wait no longer. "What is the problem we're facing?"

"Well, if I give up Sharon, which I'm prepared to do, because, as you pointed out, she's bad for Lindy and even worse for me, then I have no one to fill in on social occasions when I need a companion."

"Surely you know other women," Vanessa said.

"Not really. For the past six months I've spent twelve hours a day, six days a week, on a major acquisition that just went through, so I've sort of neglected my social life. I'm sure I'll find someone soon, but until then, what do I do?"

"I don't see how this is my problem," Vanessa protested.

"I guess it's not, but…I need help."

"I don't have any ideas."

"Look, I know it would be asking a lot, but just until I meet someone, couldn't you help me out?"

"What are you talking about?"

"Going out to dinner with me tomorrow night. I have a business meeting with a couple. I need a fourth."

"I can't—"

"So you'd rather I continued using Sharon?"

"No, but—"

"Do you have a girlfriend who'd take me on?"

"No, but— I'm sure you could find someone who will— What does she have to do, anyway?"

"Carry on a conversation with the wife so I can talk to her husband."

Vanessa looked at him in surprise. "And Sharon did that for you? I wouldn't have thought she'd be willing."

"You're right. I had to make it up to her every time. It wasn't easy. But you'd be great at it. Please, won't you help me out tomorrow night?" he repeated.

"Tomorrow night? That soon?"

"Yeah. That's why I can't find someone so quickly." He realized, waiting for her answer, how important it was to him that she agree. As if a blindfold had been ripped off his eyes, he realized how perfect she would be, and how impossible Sharon had been.

A frown creasing her forehead, Vanessa finally said, "I guess so. Just this once."

"Terrific. We'll be going to NaNa, the restaurant in the Anatole. The food there is wonderful. Do you have a cocktail dress to wear? Something chic but not too skimpy?"

"Yes, I do. I don't need you to tell me how to dress for an evening out."

Rick held up a hand. "Sorry. I didn't mean to offend."

"What will Lindy do while we're out?"

"Can't she stay here with Betty and Peter?"

"I suppose so, as long as we're not back late."

"What do you consider late?" Rick asked, watching her.

"Well, I wouldn't think dinner would take too long."

At that moment Will entered the library again, this time with his wife. Vanessa forgot their conversation at once, and bounded over to hug her mother.

After Vivian made it clear she wasn't angry at Vanessa for telling Will, she turned to their guest. "I'm glad you're still here, Rick. Will said he enjoyed talking to you."

"Same here. He certainly helped me." Rick shot Will a smile. "And your daughter has agreed to help me out tomorrow evening with a business dinner, if you don't mind our leaving Lindy here."

"I think that's very nice of Vanessa," Will said at once.

"Yes, of course." Vivian looked speculatively at her daughter, but she said nothing else.

Rick stood. "Well, I guess I should go. I've taken up a lot of your time today."

"But you haven't seen Lindy," Vanessa protested. "She'll be so disappointed if she doesn't see you."

"I'll be glad to see her—but did you tell your parents she invited me for Sunday dinner?" He looked at Vivian. "I don't want to wear out my welcome."

"That's impossible, Rick," she said, smiling genuinely. "We want Lindy to feel like she's part of the family. Any of our family is welcome on Sundays for dinner."

"I'll go up and get Lindy," Vanessa said as she moved to the door.

Rick's gaze followed her until he realized Will was speaking to him. "I'm sorry, I didn't hear what you said."

"I said, good job."

Rick smiled but shrugged. "She's just agreed to help out on an emergency basis."

"Rick!" At his sister's high-pitched voice, he turned to see her running into the room. "I didn't know you were coming over today."

"It was sort of…unplanned." He glanced at Vanessa, who came in behind his sister, but said nothing. "Did you say hello to Will and Vivian?" Rick asked Lindy softly.

"Oh, I'm sorry. I was just so excited to see you. How are you doing, Vivian? Are you feeling better?"

"Yes, dear, I am. And I heard you took care of Danny this morning when I was having a difficult time. I really appreciate that. You're a very sweet child. Have you finished shopping for the start of school?"

"She wears uniforms, Mom," Vanessa reminded her mother.

"Oh. I was going to take her shopping and buy her something nice."

"We'll talk later. I have some ideas." Vanessa smiled at her mother and Lindy.

"I don't think you should spoil her," Rick said.

Vanessa turned to him abruptly, a challenge in

her hazel eyes. "Yes, because she's been so spoiled in the past."

Rick didn't meet the challenge in her voice. Instead, he calmly explained, "No, I meant I should be the one to pay for something for Lindy."

He wasn't sure where this sudden involvement in Lindy's life had come from. Well, that wasn't true. It had come from his own conscience and from the beautiful brunette glaring at him. She had made a lot of changes in his life whether she'd intended to or not.

He thought he liked them, but he wasn't sure.

Chapter Seven

Vanessa started to answer Rick, to make her point, but her mother interrupted her. Somehow, Vanessa knew what was coming, but she couldn't figure out a way to stop it.

"Why don't you spend the rest of the afternoon here with Lindy and then have dinner with us? It will be a relaxing evening for you. And you and Vanessa can discuss anything you need to talk about. We'd love to have you stay."

"I don't think—" Rick began.

"I think it's a good idea, Rick," Will seconded. "If you get tired of visiting with the females, we can have an all-male session here in the library."

"Are you saying something about the females in this family, Will Greenfield?" Vanessa asked, her brows raised in mock censure.

"Well, you do like to talk about shopping and boys and things like that," Will said. "We men don't have much interest in those topics."

Lindy spoke up. "We could look over the choices I have to make on Monday when we visit my counselor." She glanced at Vanessa. "You need to look with us, Vanessa. You promised, remember?"

Lindy's big blue eyes were fixed on her face. How could she say no? "Uh, yes, I guess I did. Why don't the three of us move to the morning room."

"Okay!" Lindy agreed, smiling, and left to get the course booklet.

"Well," Rick said, "I guess I can do some work on Sunday, now that I'm staying for dinner this evening instead.

"Don't be silly," Vivian said at once. "We want you to come for Sunday dinner no matter what you discuss today. Lindy needs all the time she can get with you."

"That's very nice of you. I really didn't want to give up Sunday dinner," he said with a smile as he stood to follow Vanessa.

"Because you'd starve to death without Sunday dinner?" she muttered in a voice only he could hear, she hoped.

"Because I wouldn't have the charming company that I'll have here."

She grimaced but didn't respond. She didn't want her parents to think she didn't like having Rick around. She really did want him here—for Lindy's sake, of course, she hurriedly assured herself.

Lindy came back down, appearing completely happy with the arrangements.

"Here it is. She sent a copy of the four-year plan she made for me last time. Mom didn't want to look at it. I finally faked her signature because the counselor was getting upset."

"Well, that's not a problem this year," Rick said a little grimly. "With both of us at the interview and Vanessa always available for conferences even if I'm out of town, you're going to be well taken care of."

"I know. It's a nice feeling."

Vanessa gave her a hug, and they began looking at the proposed classes. It made Vanessa think about the loving care her mother had given her as she was growing up. Though her father was around, he hadn't had a lot to do with her life. It was her mother who had made sure to give her the kind of life that she now wanted Lindy to have.

"Eew!" Lindy exclaimed. "The counselor signed me up for Chinese!"

"That's good," Rick immediately said. "When I go to the Far East, it helps if I can speak even a little of their language."

"But I'm not going to China!" Lindy protested.

"You don't know that. You might join the Austin Group once you're out of college and I'd send you to China."

"I don't think so."

Before Rick could insist, Vanessa said, "She's already taking French. I think it might be better to take Spanish. They're more closely linked. Do you do business with Mexico?"

"Yes, but a lot of our business is with China and Japan."

"Perhaps Lindy could start with Spanish and if she finds it easy, next year she might add Chinese."

"I think it would be better to start it now." The look on Rick's face said he didn't intend to budge.

"Lindy, the choice is yours," Vanessa said.

"Wait a minute!" Rick countered. "She's not an adult. Doesn't my opinion count?"

"Of course it does, and you've expressed it. Now Lindy gets to make the choice."

"Good. I want to take Spanish."

"All right," Vanessa said, happy to put an end to that debate. "Let's see, the history is required, and I think you should choose the more difficult route through the mathematics since you've done so well in the past."

"But I heard business math was very helpful," Lindy said.

Vanessa shook her head. "We both know the kids who have difficulty with geometry go into business math. That's not you. You made As in math last year."

"She did?" Rick asked, surprised.

"Yes, she made straight As in her first year of high school."

"That's terrific, Lindy. Dad would've been proud of you."

Blinking rapidly so as not to show her tears, Lindy muttered, "Thanks."

Vanessa squeezed her hand. "So he should be, as well as you, Rick. She's doing the family proud."

"She is," he agreed.

"I should probably take you to the movies on Saturday evening as a reward." Vanessa smiled at Lindy.

"Good idea," Rick exclaimed. "I could take both of you. What do you want to see, Lindy?"

"There's a new Mel Gibson film coming out."

"Isn't Mel Gibson a little old for you?" Vanessa asked.

"He reminds me of Dad when he was younger, except Dad was taller."

"I've heard that's a good movie. It should be fun," Vanessa said. "But there's no need to change your plans, Rick. Lindy and I will be fine alone."

"Oh, no, you're not leaving me out of the fun. I don't have any other plans." He smiled at Lindy, who enthusiastically nodded.

Vanessa was kicking herself for suggesting such a thing in front of Rick. Now she was having dinner with him tonight and tomorrow night and going to the movies with him on Saturday. She could think of only one other way to rid herself of him.

"But Lindy and I will probably go to an early movie."

"That's fine with me. In fact, it's great, because then I can take the two of you out to dinner afterward."

"Oh, that would be so much fun!" Lindy exclaimed, and Vanessa knew she was trapped.

"Well, now that we've finished our consultation, I guess you can join Will in the library. I think I heard Mom going up to check on Danny a few minutes ago."

Rick grinned at her, as if he could read her mind. "I'll be happy to. Is it a relief to have me out of the way?"

"I just wanted you to feel comfortable. You made yourself quite plain on that subject."

"I believe that was Will, not me, who suggested some male bonding. But I'll be pleased to join him. I found him quite wise the last time we visited."

Vanessa frowned. What had Rick talked to Will about? Did it have anything to do with her going out with him tomorrow night? She reminded herself to talk to Will herself as soon as she got rid of Rick, which apparently wasn't going to happen anytime soon.

Rick stood and leaned over to kiss Lindy's cheek. "I'll see you at dinner, Lindy." He looked at Vanessa as if he was going to give her a kiss on the cheek, too. She glared at him, hoping to convey her reluctance. Apparently, she did a good job because he just smiled and walked out of the room.

"Oh, isn't Rick being great?" Lindy asked.

Vanessa knew what Lindy wanted to hear and she supplied it. "Yes, he's being very cooperative."

"Saturday will be so much fun!"

"I could stay home and let you have Rick all to yourself," Vanessa suggested.

"I think Rick would be disappointed," Lindy said, staring at Vanessa.

"But that would be my third dinner with him in a row."

Lindy frowned. "You're having dinner with him tomorrow night?"

Vanessa explained about him needing a companion, now that he'd dropped Sharon.

"Do you think he's falling in love with you?"

Vanessa was shocked by the thought. She denied it vehemently. "Sweetie, adults don't fall in and out of love as much as teenagers do. Your brother is a busy man. This is business, that's all. He probably won't pay any attention to me."

"But it's okay if he does fall in love with you, because I know you love me, too."

Vanessa hugged the girl. "Absolutely right. I love you. You're my little sister and will always be my little sister. But sisterly love is a lot less complicated than that man-woman thing." Vanessa paused. "Oh, I don't think I told you the big news of the day. Mom's pregnant again."

"She is?" Lindy asked, her eyes big. "That's wonderful."

"So you may not be my only little sister."

Lindy grinned. "I don't mind. I like babies."

"They are sweet. But they have some drawbacks. Dirty diapers, not sleeping all night. Luckily, Mom has help. But my sister Rebecca was unmarried and alone when she had Joey. It was quite a struggle for her."

"Why wasn't Jeff around? He seems very nice."

"It's a long story, but he moved before he knew she was pregnant and lost touch with her. When we finally located her, in Arkansas, Mom talked her into coming here for a week. Then we managed to keep her with us. Mom found her a job in her lawyer's office. He had recently died, but his nephew had taken over. And that was Jeff."

"So they had a happy reunion?"

"Not at first. At the time Jeff was engaged to Chelsea."

"But she's his partner's wife."

"Yeah. Tricky, huh?"

Lindy sighed, grinning. "Yes, but it always seems to come right with your family."

"We've been fortunate, I guess. Rebecca's twin, Rachel, got really sick, but that turned out well, too, because she was reunited with J.D. and they fell in love."

"That's what I mean. I hope I'm as lucky when I grow up," Lindy said.

"Me, too, honey. Me, too."

VANESSA CHECKED her appearance in the full-length mirror on the back of her bedroom door. She was wearing her favorite black dinner dress with a string of pearls and matching earrings. Her nails were painted crimson and her dark hair fell around her face in waves.

A knock interrupted her appraisal. She opened the door to Lindy.

"Oh, you look beautiful."

"Thanks, sweetie."

"Is it okay if I come downstairs to see Rick before you go?" the girl asked.

"Of course, if you're not tired of him by now."

Vanessa had been teasing, but Lindy didn't seem to realize it. "Are *you* getting tired of him?" she asked, her expression suddenly anxious.

"No, honey, I was just kidding. You've seen him a lot this week."

"Yeah, but tomorrow he's taking us to the movies and to dinner. I've never done that before."

Vanessa sometimes forgot Lindy's history because she was fitting in so well with the family. But then she said something like that. "Of course, and we'll have a wonderful time," Vanessa said.

"What should I wear for tomorrow night?" Lindy loved having choices now that she owned some nice clothes.

"You can wear your new slacks with that pretty blouse we bought, or you might want to put that blouse with one of your casual skirts."

They both heard the distant ring of the doorbell. Lindy jumped up from Vanessa's bed. "I'll go say hi to Rick."

"Of course. Tell him I'll be right down."

Vanessa let out a sigh of relief that she had a moment alone before she faced Rick. In spite of her determination to ignore the man, she was going out with him tonight, as his date. She knew she should remain completely unaffected by his presence, but she was finding it difficult. Which was a ridiculous admission for someone who had studied people's behavior for years.

She took a deep breath. She was going to be friendly yet distant, sophisticated yet relaxed.

Right! At least she was going to give it a try.

RICK WASN'T SURPRISED to be shown into the morning room and told Vanessa would be down soon. Women were often late. Sharon used to keep him waiting a minimum of half an hour.

When the door opened, he looked up in surprise to find his half sister. "Lindy! I didn't know I'd get to see you tonight. How are you doing?"

The child ran over and hugged his neck. It amazed him how good that hug felt. Like they were a family again.

"I'm fine. Vanessa will be down in a minute. I just wanted to say hi. You haven't forgotten our plans for tomorrow, have you?"

"No, of course not."

"I'm so excited. I've never been to a movie theater before and Mom didn't take me out to eat, ever."

Rick again felt that jolt of regret. "Don't worry,

kiddo," he said, hugging her again. "You're going to experience a lot of new things this year. Pretty soon, you'll become blasé about an evening spent with your brother."

"I'm sure you're wrong," she said, looking starry-eyed.

Rick knew he wasn't wrong, but he appreciated her enthusiasm for his company right now. "What will you do this evening, while we're out?"

"Oh, Rebecca and Jeff are coming over for dinner and I'll get to play with their kids."

"Well, don't wait up for us. I'm not sure when we'll get back."

"I won't. Vanessa doesn't like me to stay up late."

"She's not too hard on you, is she?"

Lindy looked at him like he was crazy. "Vanessa?"

As if that had been her cue, Vanessa entered the room. Rick automatically looked at his watch.

"I'm sorry if I kept you waiting," she said stiffly.

He looked up and the words lodged in his throat. She was beautiful. He'd never seen her dressed up and he liked what he saw now. The cocktail dress was tasteful yet sexy; the makeup was understated and enhanced her natural beauty.

He nearly stuttered, but regrouped in time to say, "You didn't keep me waiting. Lindy and I were just chatting."

The doorbell rang again and Lindy headed toward the door. "That will be Rebecca and Jeff."

Her exit left an awkward silence in the morning room.

He felt the need to explain himself. "I wasn't being critical when I looked at my watch. I actually expected you to be a lot later. Sharon always was."

"I'm not Sharon."

Well, that excuse hadn't gotten him anywhere, Rick decided. But she had a point. She looked better than Sharon could ever hope to look. "Definitely not. Do you want to visit with Rebecca and Jeff before we go?"

"No, thank you."

"Okay." He moved to her side and took her arm, but she jerked away from his touch.

He stood back until she went out the door, then followed. He had a feeling it was going to be a long night.

In the hallway, he greeted Jeff and his wife and children. Vanessa hugged her sister and whispered something in her ear. Then she excused herself and exited. With raised eyebrows, he followed her.

On their way down the walk, he asked, "Am I allowed to open the car door for you?"

"Yes" was her terse reply.

He'd intended to tell her how nice she looked, but he wouldn't chance that until she was trapped in the car. She slid into the front seat of his Mercedes and he closed the door. Then he circled the car to get behind the wheel.

After driving away from her home, he finally ventured a compliment. "You look lovely tonight, Vanessa."

"Thank you, but that's not necessary."

"What's not necessary?"

"Flattery. I'm doing this as a favor to you. You don't have to try to make me feel like you wanted me here."

What could he say? She was right. He had made it seem as if she was doing him a favor. Truthfully, though, if Vanessa eased up, he could enjoy the dinner more than he ever had with Sharon. No doubt his business associates would, too. But he couldn't tell her that.

They rode in silence for a while, until he said, "The couple we're meeting tonight is in town from Los Angeles. He's interviewing for a job with my company and has received favorable reviews from upper management. If all goes well tonight, I'll offer him a job."

"I see. What role does his wife play? Do you want me to sell her on Dallas?"

"I don't know. I haven't heard that she has an opinion. Certainly, it wouldn't hurt to make Dallas sound attractive."

"Do they have children?"

"Two, ages two and six months."

"And their names?"

"John and Hillary Williams."

"All right. I'll do what I can to keep her entertained."

He felt as if she were a trained agent whom he'd just briefed on a target's secret dossier. She was all business, focused and determined. He wished she'd lighten up. But he nodded and said, "Good. I appreciate it."

After several more minutes of silence, he asked, "Have you ever been to NaNa?"

"No, I haven't. I don't go out that often."

He turned to her and was stunned again by how beautiful she was. She was a knockout. Why weren't men beating down her door for a chance to be with her? Or maybe they were. He realized he didn't even know if she was dating someone.

And why did he care?

He struggled to focus on the conversation. Where were they? Oh, yes. "Why not?"

She let out a huff. "I have a busy life, Rick. I'm working on my doctorate and teaching three classes at the university. And I have my family. They're very important to me."

"I'm sure, but—"

"I was raised an only child. I have Danny now, as you have Lindy, but after my dad died, it was just me and Mom. When I found out I had siblings, I wanted to meet them so badly."

"Yeah, I guess you would. Did Will find them quickly?"

"Well, he found Rebecca first, but he also fell in love with Mom, so that slowed things down a little," Vanessa said with a laugh.

Rick was relieved to see her softening a little. "So that's how they met?"

"Yes, but Will was prejudiced against rich people."

"Why?"

"Because his first wife had left him to marry an old man just because he was rich."

"Sounds like my dear stepmother," Rick said.

"And Sharon," Vanessa added.

He glanced over at her, but she was staring straight ahead. "How did your mom straighten Will out?"

"She didn't even try. She was too interested in finding my siblings. When Will saw that she put my happiness above any material things, he realized she was different."

"Will mentioned that your brother Jim and someone named Alex work for him. I haven't met them."

"Jim is wonderful, the big brother all little girls dream of," Vanessa said.

"Then I definitely need to meet him, so I'll know what kind of brother I need to be for Lindy."

Vanessa continued, "And Alex is my other brother David's wife. She was a police officer before she joined Will's firm."

"How did she meet your brother?"

"Oh, she knew David before. They're cousins."

"She married her cousin?"

"Yes, but they're not really cousins. I mean, David was adopted by her uncle and his wife. So they were legally cousins, but not blood cousins."

"Okay," he said, drawing out the word. "That still seems a little odd to me."

Vanessa went on the defensive. "Well, it's not!"

"I know, I know. Your family is perfect." He let a little sarcasm slip into his voice. He knew he shouldn't, but he was tired of being the bad guy.

"I didn't mean that. It's just— You don't know them."

"You're right, but I'd like to meet them. Will they be there on Sunday?"

"I'm not sure. Sometimes they come. And David's little sister, his adopted sister, and her husband come sometimes, too."

"Man, you must have a real crowd on Sundays."

"We do. That's how Mom and I like it. We wish Rachel and J.D. lived closer, but they don't." As if suddenly remembering, she added, "Rachel is my sister Rebecca's twin."

"Twin? Are they identical?"

"They are. But neither of them knew she had a twin. It was amazing when we helped them find each other. And wonderful for me. Suddenly I had two sisters where I'd had none."

Rick smiled at her. "It's a good thing you had a lot of siblings to find—it's obvious you were meant for a big family."

"Yes, I was."

"We're picking them up here," he said as he pulled into the driveway of the hotel where the Williamses were staying. He regretted that they had to entertain someone else this evening. He realized he'd rather spend the time with Vanessa alone.

For a lot of reasons.

"You want to come in with me while I get them or wait here in the car?"

"I'll just wait here, if it's all right."

Inside the hotel, he saw the Williamses waiting for him. Again he considered how much better the evening was going to be with Vanessa instead of Sharon as his companion. These people had no idea how lucky they were. If he was right, though, they soon would.

Chapter Eight

It didn't take long for Vanessa to show her value as his date for the evening. As soon as they were all settled in the car and on their way, introductions over, she engaged the couple in conversation. She was well spoken, intelligent, friendly. Simply put, she charmed them.

When they arrived at the Anatole, they took the elevator up to NaNa's, and the maître d' showed them to their table, which had a great view of downtown.

"It's so good to be back in Dallas," Hillary said as they were seated.

"I didn't realize you'd been to Dallas before," Rick noted.

"Oh, yes, I was raised here."

"You didn't care for L.A.?" he asked. The couple had been living there since their marriage.

"Well, at first it was exciting. I did all the tourist things. But after a while, the excitement died away and I realized it was just a much-too-big town with a lot of smog. It's true there was a beach nearby and mountains not too far away, but we had children to consider. It was like living with a chain smoker."

"I hadn't thought of it that way." Vanessa glanced at Rick, as if waiting for him to comment.

"That's an unusual take on L.A.," he said, and looked at John. "Did you like L.A.?"

"I did when I went to school out there. But I was young and single then. Now I have two children and Hillary needs some help on the weekends."

"You realize this job would involve travel?" Rick asked.

Hillary answered before John could. "Yes, but my family is here. If I needed help, they'd come. Out there, the only person we could call on was our neighbor and...well, she had the hots for John."

"Now, honey, there's no need to tell Rick all our problems," John said hurriedly, anxiety obvious under his forced laugh.

Vanessa immediately stepped in and changed the subject, much to Rick's relief. "Well, I guess I don't have to sell you on Dallas, since you're already from here. It's a great city, isn't it?"

Fortunately, the waiter arrived to take their drink orders and tell them the specials.

"Everything sounds wonderful," Hillary said when he left. "With the kids we don't go out much, and when we do it's nothing fancy like this."

Rick smiled at her obvious delight. "Then I'm

glad we're all out tonight. This restaurant is famous, and rightly so."

Vanessa was surprised to find herself appreciating Rick's easy manner and how quickly he made the Williamses so comfortable. They'd come close to disaster a few minutes earlier. She'd done her best to steer the conversation in the right direction, but it was Rick who set the tone now. In no time they were all relaxing over drinks.

She was actually enjoying herself, but she'd also warmed to their conversation in the car earlier. And now she was finding more depth to Rick and appreciating his ease in social situations.

Which made her nervous.

She began to see him as a danger zone. For one, he was way too handsome. But she'd assumed, as with other good-looking men, that he would be fixated on himself, and much to her surprise, he seemed more interested in other people. And for another, his attention to her was too flattering. An inner voice kept telling her not to be affected but wasn't sure she was heeding the warning.

"Honey, have you decided what you'll have?"

She looked up in surprise. Was Rick talking to her?

With his dark eyes gazing into hers, she suddenly lost her train of thought. She swallowed back a gulp and somehow remembered something on the menu. The endearment meant nothing, she told herself. They were playing their roles.

The foursome chatted during the appetizers, Vanessa telling Hillary how Dallas had changed since she'd moved away. Her occupying the spouse gave Rick an opportunity to speak to John about the Austin Group. From what Vanessa overheard, she thought John had a good grasp of the corporation.

"How long have you two been dating?"

She almost choked on a shrimp at Hillary's question. What was she supposed to answer?

Fortunately Rick had heard the question and turned to answer. "Not long," he said. "I just met her a couple of weeks ago."

"Really? You two seem so in tune to each other's needs, it's amazing it's been such a short relationship," Hillary said. "You seem as comfortable together as we are."

"I don't think Rick needs any encouragement, Hillary," Vanessa hurriedly said. "He knows me for what I am."

Both John and Hillary looked at Rick.

"I can assure you I'm moving as fast as I can," Rick said with a smile. "But Vanessa is a lady who won't be rushed, no matter how much I try." He winked.

"How true," Vanessa said smoothly, ignoring the gesture.

To her relief, the waiter appeared with their meals and the conversation turned to food.

THEY HAD MOVED ON TO COFFEE and dessert when Rick noticed something different about the evening. This was the part of the meal where Sharon would have been flirting either with him or with John, making their conversation impossible. Instead, Vanessa sat through story after story about Hillary's children, even endured their baby pictures, all the time looking interested.

Just as he was counting his blessings, he caught some movement over Hillary's shoulder.

It couldn't be.

It was.

Sharon was talking to the maître d' and pointing at their table.

He leaned in close to Vanessa, inhaling the smell of her perfume, and whispered, "Sharon."

In tune with him, she discreetly glanced over to the front of the restaurant. Without so much as a frown she whispered back, "Intercept her. She's here to make trouble."

In his best business tone, Rick said to everyone at the table, "Excuse me, please." He got up and crossed the room to where a determined Sharon was zeroing in on her target.

Vanessa did her best to keep the Williamses' attention. She wouldn't allow Sharon to ruin Rick's business dinner. She turned to the young couple. "So, tell me, does your son get along with the baby?"

Hillary talked for several minutes, with John

adding some interesting anecdotes. Rick was back before they knew it.

"I beg your pardon," he said as he sat down, nodding at Vanessa in a secret code that told her everything was under control. "Now, where were we? Yes, I remember. I was just about to offer John the position."

Once he accepted, and Hillary discussed her moving plans, they were ready to drive the couple back to their hotel.

"Nice job this evening," Rick said as soon as he and Vanessa were alone in the car.

"Thanks, but I didn't do much."

"Nonsense, you had to endure two hours of baby stories." He grinned widely.

Vanessa laughed. "It was a good thing you waylaid Sharon before she got to the table. What did you say to her, anyway?"

"I paid her off," he said succinctly. Then he continued. "A pair of diamond earrings is cheap compared to what she would've cost me. John's a great fit for my team."

After a few seconds Vanessa said, "It was nice of you to offer John a signing bonus."

"I really thought he deserved it. He'll make it back for me. And a little extra cash is handy when you're moving."

"How do you know that?" Vanessa asked curiously. "You're still living in the family home, aren't you?"

"Yeah, just like you. We actually have a lot in common."

"I don't think so."

"Oh yeah? We both live at home, neither of us is starving to death, are we?"

"No, but that's where the similarity ends."

He wished he weren't driving so he could look at her and gauge her expression. Was she offended that he'd said something about her still living at home? Truth be told, she was right—that was where the similarities between them ended. She was warm and gregarious and family-oriented, while he... Well, suffice to say he was none of those things. The only thing he cared about was work.

But that was changing, he realized. Hadn't he missed yesterday's meetings? In ten years that was a first. But he couldn't tell Vanessa that. So instead, he agreed.

"Yeah, you're probably right. But I know I owe you for offering such a lovely toast to our business agreement. John was impressed, too. It made for a perfect ending to a long night."

"Okay, I'll agree you owe me for that one." She sighed. "As much as I enjoyed the meal, I was ready for the evening to end."

He knew she meant because of the endless baby stories. "That makes two of us."

Typical of Vanessa, she excused Hillary Williams. "Having two babies so close together can shift your emphasis to them and nothing else. I hope I don't ever get that self-absorbed."

"You won't," he assured her with a smile. "But I'm not sure how you managed to grow up so unselfcentered as an only child. Didn't your parents spoil you?"

"No, not really. Dad didn't pay me much attention, and Mom believed in encouraging me to use whatever time I had to improve myself."

"Do you think she'll be the same with Danny and the new one?"

"Of course," Vanessa said. "Danny has already taken karate and gone on playdates. This year he's going to prekindergarten."

"He's very young. Don't you think she's expecting too much?"

"Not at all. Mom went through everything I did herself. She watched my gymnastics lessons, my soccer games, my school concerts. She took me out to lunch once a week so I would learn to use good manners. She was a wonderful mother."

"I'm not saying she wasn't. Obviously you're a living example of how good she is."

"Thank you—I think."

He could feel her studying him now in the darkness of the car. "It was definitely a compliment."

"I told you before, Rick, that compliments aren't necessary."

She was wrong. He wanted to pull the Mercedes over to the side of the road, get out of the car so he could see her face in the moonlight when he gave the compliments she deserved. He had to satisfy himself with a sideways glance.

"You've got it all wrong, Vanessa. You earned compliments the minute you walked into the morning room. You earned more by your charming behavior tonight. You totally won over the Williamses. And me." What was he saying? He glanced her way again; she didn't seem to react, so he pressed on. "You look beautiful."

When she spoke, her voice sounded thick, as if she hadn't spoken in a while. "You—looked very nice tonight, too." She cleared her throat. "But I think I'd like to see you in something other than a suit. It always makes you look a little stuffy."

He laughed. "Well, I think I can give you a new look for tomorrow night when we take Lindy out." That put him in mind of his sister. "I can hardly believe she's never been to a movie and dinner."

"I know. She fits in so well that I forget that she lived such a desperate life."

"We'll start by making it up to her tomorrow night," Rick said as he parked the car in front of Vanessa's home. Even though the suggestion had come from Vanessa and he'd invited himself along, he felt good about their plans with Lindy.

Before she could step out of the car, Rick got out and came around to help her.

"Really, this isn't necessary."

He smiled at her. "My mother taught me good manners. Always to the door."

"I wasn't sure how much you remembered her. You've never mentioned her."

"I remember her. She died when I was fifteen years old. Dad remarried when I was sixteen. Somehow my stepmother did not replace my mother in my mind."

"No, I think I can see that," Vanessa said as they walked to her door.

Anita was one subject he didn't want to talk about. "Yeah. Well, I checked the time for the movie Lindy wanted to see. I'll need to pick the two of you up around three, then we'll go to dinner afterward. Do you have any preferences?"

"No, as long as it's not fast food."

"I think we can do a little better than that, no matter what Lindy says. She can use her allowance for that."

"I'll tell her you said that." Vanessa gave a teasing smile.

He was smiling back at her as Vanessa turned to open the door. But he wasn't prepared for the evening to end like that.

He felt that he'd gotten to know her, to sense the warmth that Will had talked about. He'd seen her go out of her way to make things easier for both him and the other couple. And she didn't expect any kind of a reward, not even compliments, though she'd richly deserved heaps of them.

He was so amazed with her that he didn't want to let her go. He knew he had to; however, he didn't intend to let her escape without something—something that he wanted badly. So he swung her back around, leaned over and kissed her.

Chapter Nine

"Vanessa, aren't you ready yet?" Lindy called as she ran into Vanessa's bedroom.

"Calm down, Lindy. It's only ten to three."

"You're still coming, aren't you?"

"I told you I would," Vanessa said calmly. She'd tried to talk her way out of the plans, but Lindy would have none of it. She said she'd stay home if Vanessa did. Vanessa couldn't deny Lindy her pleasure, so she caved in.

But she'd learned something last night. Not only was Rick dangerous, but he couldn't be trusted to keep his distance. Her alert level had shot from yellow to blazing red when he kissed her.

If he wouldn't keep any distance between them, *she* would have to. She'd go tonight, because she had Lindy to protect her. After that, she wouldn't leave the house with the man.

"He's here!" Lindy announced so that everyone in the house could hear her.

Vanessa drew in a deep breath. Of course, he was here early. "Lindy, you must calm down. This is only the first of many outings."

"I'll go down and greet him, okay?"

Vanessa nodded and watched the teenager run down the stairs. She didn't have much choice but to follow. She mentally arranged her full body armor and stepped out into the danger zone.

"WHERE'S VANESSA?" Rick asked as Lindy came into the morning room alone.

"She's coming. She said I should calm down, but I'm so excited, Rick!"

He gave his little sister a hug. "I can see that. After today you may not think going out is so much fun, so I think you should enjoy it."

"That's what I think, too!" She beamed at him.

He laughed and then glanced at the door. "You're sure she's coming?"

"Yes, she promised me. She said she was tired and didn't think she'd go, but I told her I wouldn't go without her."

"I see. You mean you would've stood me up?"

"Not really, but Vanessa is—is my strength. She always shows me how I should behave. And I want her to enjoy today, too."

"So do I, Lindy. We'll show her we Austins know how to have fun, won't we."

"Yeah!"

"What are you agreeing to, Lindy?" Vanessa asked from the doorway.

"Nothing you would object to," Rick hurriedly said. "We were saying that we Austins would show you we know how to have fun."

"I see." There was no smile attached to her words.

"Are you ready to go?" Rick asked, hoping to get her into the car before she had a chance to change her mind.

"Yes, of course."

As they walked down the hall, Vanessa stepped to the door of the kitchen. "Betty? Lindy and I are going out with Rick. We'll be back after dinner."

"But I have plenty fixed," Betty said.

"You're feeding me tomorrow, Betty. I need to feel I'm doing my share," Rick said over Vanessa's head. He winked at Betty and she smiled, satisfied.

Rick escorted his two ladies out to the car. He opened the back door for Lindy, though Vanessa protested that she should be the one in the backseat.

"We're going with age before beauty today, my dear," Rick said before winking at Lindy.

"Vanessa's the prettiest," Lindy said staunchly.

"Well, I'd say it's a close race."

Vanessa remained silent on the ride to the movie theater. There was no enjoyable conversation such as they'd shared last night. And when they entered the theater, she insisted on having Lindy sit in the middle, between them, saying that that way, they could both share in her excitement.

Rick wasn't fooled. He knew the reason for Vanessa's coolness. She was upset that he'd kissed her last night.

It hadn't been a long kiss, or a deep kiss. It had been a chaste salute for a job well done. A demonstration of affection for a woman he was beginning to appreciate much more than he'd expected.

It had also been a mistake.

He hadn't realized how much that kiss would awaken a hunger to repeat the move. Hell, he'd kissed Sharon much more intimately, but most of those kisses had been instigated by her and had left him cold. One simple kiss with Vanessa and he found himself longing for more.

But she was sending him a message by her behavior today. *Keep your distance.*

Unwilling to accept his dismissal, he stretched his arm around Lindy after the theater darkened, letting his hand rest on the edge of Vanessa's seat. He knew it was contrary, but he enjoyed thinking that his behavior upset her.

When the lights finally came on, Lindy still sat there, not moving.

"Lindy, are you okay?" Rick asked.

"Yes, but—but wasn't that amazing?"

Rick looked at Vanessa and, to his surprise, she met his gaze with a smile. "Uh, well, it wasn't too bad."

"Honey, you'll get more used to seeing movies in

a while. There are better movies, I promise." Vanessa patted her charge on her back.

"There are?"

Rick chuckled. "Yeah. Come on." He moved to the end of the row and then stood back for the ladies to precede him. Which, of course, meant Vanessa would be immediately in front of him. He couldn't think of any reason to touch her, as much as he wanted to.

They came out into the sunlight, blinking several times to deal with the brightness. When they reached the car, Lindy naturally took the backseat again. Vanessa glared at Rick and he lifted his hands in innocence.

He backed out of the parking space and then said over his shoulder to Lindy, "I made us a reservation at a restaurant I thought you'd enjoy."

"Where is it?"

"It's called The Dragonfly. It's in a hotel off McKinney Avenue."

"It's well known for its diverse clientele," Vanessa added, smiling at Lindy.

"Have you been there?" Lindy asked.

"Yes, a couple of times."

"I should've known," Rick said. "I bet there's not a restaurant in town you haven't been to."

"That's not true. I hadn't been to NaNa's until last night," Vanessa replied.

"I'm glad to be one of your firsts," he said with a big grin.

Her chilly air returned and she looked out her window.

Lindy was properly awed by the restaurant. Though she might've preferred a good hamburger, she willingly tried whatever they served.

By the time they left the restaurant, it was dark.

"Wow, I didn't realize we were in there for so long," Lindy exclaimed.

"Fine dining takes time," Rick said as they got into his car.

"Of course, it wouldn't have taken quite as long if we'd passed up the dessert," Vanessa said. "I'm going to have to exercise a lot to get rid of those calories."

"I think you'll be fine," Rick assured her.

She sent him the dirty look he was beginning to think was the only way she ever looked at him. "Easy for you to say."

"And here I was going to suggest we stop off for ice cream on the way home," Rick teased.

"Even I'm not interested in ice cream tonight," Lindy said with a sigh. "But tonight was so much fun. Thank you both for making it happen."

Again Rick and Vanessa exchanged glances. He knew that in his mind the evening had become about him and Vanessa, but it wasn't really about that. It was about Lindy doing what most teenagers had done when they were three. Going to the movies for the first time and then to dinner with family.

They both looked at Lindy.

"It was my pleasure, little sister," Rick said.

"Yes, it was fun, honey. And you're going to do a lot more things. We want to make up for those nine years with your mother," Vanessa said.

"I don't think she meant to be mean," Lindy said hesitantly. "She was just busy."

Vanessa seemed to force herself to smile. "Maybe you're right, but you've missed out on a lot."

Rick stopped the car in front of their house, then got out and opened Lindy's door. He started around the back of the car to open Vanessa's door, but she was already out, and passed by him.

"Thank you for today, Rick," she said politely before he could turn to walk them to the door.

"My pleasure," he said, then motioned to the house. "Shall we?"

"It's not necessary. We'll see you tomorrow after church."

He got the message. But he couldn't help teasing her. "Here's your hat—what's your hurry?"

"I just assumed you'd be pleased to—"

"What?" he asked.

With her gaze on Lindy, Vanessa said, "I assumed you had other things you needed to do, but, of course, you're welcome to come in for coffee. I would guess Rebecca and Jeff are still here, too."

Rick had noticed Lindy's stare. "Thanks, I'd enjoy some coffee. I've had such a nice time, I hate for this day to end." He put an arm around Lindy, and they followed Vanessa to the front door.

When she opened it, Peter appeared in the hallway.

"Hi, Peter. Are Rebecca and Jeff still here?"

"Yes, they're all in the morning room. Shall I bring more coffee?"

"Yes, please."

"Oh, good, I get to see Jamie and Joey as well as Danny," Lindy said, rushing ahead.

Rick put a hand on Vanessa's arm. "Good catch back there. We almost ruined a fun day for Lindy."

"Yes, I hadn't thought— She was watching us, horrified."

"Yeah. But I think you made everything all right. I appreciate it, on Lindy's behalf."

Vanessa took a deep breath. "Let's go get coffee."

For a little while, at least, they were on the same side.

MONDAY WAS THE FIFTH DAY in a row that Vanessa would spend time with Rick Austin. Considering she hadn't known him but two weeks, she thought the constant association with him was a little over the top. Besides, he was occupying too much of her mind, and that was becoming a problem.

Today they were going to the appointment with Lindy's counselor at the private high school she attended. Vanessa had dressed to impress, choosing a cream-colored suit in linen that showed off her dark hair. To impress the counselor, of course. Not Rick.

Lindy was dressed in one of her new blouses and a pretty skirt. Together they went downstairs to await Rick. They didn't want to be late.

When Rick pulled up, they dashed out the front door and got into the car before he could make a move to get out.

"Are we late?" he asked with a frown.

"No, but we don't want to be," Lindy said from the passenger seat. "She almost gave up on me last year. I want to show her how everything has improved."

"I think just looking at you two would convince her. You make me proud," Rick said, his gaze wandering to Vanessa in the rearview mirror.

"Are we going?" Vanessa reminded him, since they were still parked at the curb.

"Right now." He pulled away, grinning.

When they reached the school, Lindy guided them to the counselor's office. Lindy knocked on the door and walked in. "Hello, Mrs. Wilkie."

"Why, Lindy, don't you look nice." The tall woman stood to greet them.

Rick stepped forward. "I'm Lindy's brother, Rick Austin."

Vanessa was waiting to introduce herself when the woman said, "I'm so glad you and your wife were able to come. Last year, it seemed like no one cared about Lindy."

Rick immediately said, "She's not my wife."

At the same time, Vanessa said, "I'm not his wife."

Mrs. Wilkie blinked. "Girlfriend?"

They both said, "No!"

Vanessa decided to take charge. "I'm Vanessa Shaw, Lindy's temporary guardian. Because Mr. Austin travels a great deal, we thought it would be better for Lindy to live with me until she's older."

"Oh. I'm sure that will be a good arrangement. Last year I could never reach her mother."

Vanessa smiled. "I'll be available or someone at my home will know where to find me. Before we leave I'll give you numbers where you can reach me."

"I'll give you my numbers, too," Rick said. "Though, of course, Vanessa will call me if it's anything serious anyway."

Mrs. Wilkie seemed pleased. "Won't you all be seated?"

They began to go over Lindy's choices, Vanessa leaving it up to Lindy to explain what they'd decided.

Before they finished, Rick's cell phone rang. "Uh, I'll just step outside to take this call," he said hurriedly and slipped out of the room.

He still hadn't returned when they ended the interview. Vanessa led Lindy outside, wondering if they would find Rick out there, still on the phone.

He was there, pacing back and forth, talking fast.

Vanessa frowned. Were they supposed to stand around and wait for him?

He saw them and waved for them to come along as he headed to the car. It didn't appear he intended to end his call. When they reached the car, Vanessa went to the driver's side and held out her hand for the keys.

Surprising her, he dropped the keys into her hand and went around to the passenger side.

While Rick spoke on the cell phone, Vanessa drove the short distance to her house and parked the car. Just as she did so, Rick ended his conversation.

"I need to come in and talk to both of you," he said, his expression serious.

"Is something wrong?" Lindy asked in an anxious voice.

"Come on, Lindy. He'll explain when we get inside," Vanessa said.

When they were settled in the library, she asked Rick, "What is it?"

"I've been offered the opportunity to join a government group on a trip to China. It means I'll be gone for three weeks. I won't even be able to call you during that time. We'll be moving around a lot in areas that are fairly primitive."

"Why do you want to go?" Lindy asked.

Vanessa took her hand, recognizing some fear in the girl's voice.

"Lindy, it's an opportunity to expand into a country that has the biggest population in the world. I can't pass this up."

"But—"

Vanessa reached out and took Lindy's hand. "Sweetie, we'll be okay without your brother for three weeks. You'll be safe and loved. That's why he's letting you live with me."

"I know," Lindy said, her voice small.

Rick knelt in front of her. "Honey, I know I'll miss you, but it will establish our company, Dad's company, as one of the premier ones in the world. Dad would be so proud."

"Me, too, I'm proud," Lindy said as she hugged his neck.

Vanessa saw on Rick's face that he was touched by her words and courage.

"I love you, Lindy," he said.

"I love you, too."

He smiled at her. "I need to talk to Vanessa before I go. Why don't you go on upstairs?"

Lindy nodded and left the room.

"Yes?" Vanessa said, drawing his attention back to her.

"I'm going to check with Jeff and make sure the money and power of attorney are all in place. Is there anything else you need?"

"No, I don't think so."

He pulled her to her feet. "Then I guess all I have to do is tell you goodbye."

"Good—" Before she could get the word out, he pulled her against him and kissed her. And it was not the kind of chaste kiss he'd given her on Friday night.

As she'd known in her heart, such close contact with the man was dangerous—because it made her want more. And she didn't intend to get involved just yet. She pushed herself away. "Why did you do that?" she demanded.

"So you wouldn't forget me while I'm away," he whispered. "Take care of Lindy."

"Of course," she muttered, and found herself wrapped in his arms for a hug. Then he was gone.

She should've gone up to Lindy at once. Instead, she went to one of the front windows to watch him drive away.

"You all right, Vanessa?" Betty asked, coming up behind her.

"Oh! Yes. Have you got a nice snack for Lindy? She's a little upset. Her brother just left for three weeks."

"Why, that poor little thing. I'll fix a tray and bring it up right away. You go see about her. I'll take care of everything."

Vanessa hugged Betty and thanked her. Then she hurried upstairs, wishing a snack would fix what was wrong with her.

THE NEXT TWENTY-FOUR HOURS for Rick were nonstop as he packed in a rush and made his way to the airport to fly to Washington for a quick indoctrination for the trip to China. He was given enough reading material to keep him busy all during the long flight overseas.

So why did his mind keep returning to those few

minutes with Lindy in the Greenfields' library? He hadn't realized how much being reunited with his baby sister would mean to him. It was as if she'd restored his father to him. The three of them had shared a lot for the first six years of her life. Then her mother had driven him away. Or he'd allowed himself to be driven away.

He should've fought for his father and Lindy. And he hadn't. Now he was being given a second chance to reunite his family, even though it now consisted only of him and Lindy.

He could still feel her young arms around his neck as he told her he loved her. And she'd responded in kind. Family was important. He realized now that he'd felt hollow since his dad's death. Alone and not significant to anyone else's life.

He also remembered the kiss he'd given Vanessa. It had taken her a minute to push away. In that minute he'd realized he didn't want to leave her. She was beginning to mean a hell of a lot to him.

In three weeks he'd be back. Then he could see her and make her understand what he was feeling. For the first time in his life, he thought he might be falling in love. And he liked it.

VANESSA ARRIVED HOME after teaching her first class, glad to settle back into a routine she loved. Lindy had started school a week ago, just after Rick left. The homework kept her occupied in the evenings, which helped pass the time before her brother came home.

As Vanessa started upstairs, Betty came out of the kitchen and called her. "You have a visitor. She insisted on waiting."

Something in Betty's voice warned Vanessa that she was not going to like what was about to happen. She entered the library to find Sharon sitting there with a bored look on her face, sporting some new diamond earrings.

"Hello, Sharon."

"Oh. You're finally here. I need to know how to get in touch with Rick. The people at his company won't tell me anything."

"Why do you need to talk to Rick?"

"Because I've just found out I'm pregnant!"

Chapter Ten

Vanessa stared at the woman. All the warm feelings she'd had for Rick Austin suddenly turned cold.

Tamping down her emotions, she said in a professional tone, "I'm afraid he can't be reached right now."

"Why not?"

"He's in China with a group from the government."

"China? You're just making that up!" Sharon challenged.

Vanessa didn't react. "I have no reason to lie to you. Have you been to a doctor?"

"That's none of your business." She stood up. "Where is his sister?"

"She's in school, of course."

"Well, I think I should tell her that I'll soon be her sister-in-law."

"I don't think you should pass on your fantasy to Lindy. When her brother returns, *if* he wants to introduce you as his fiancée, then you can see Lindy."

"You don't think he'll marry me? He bought me these earrings." She pointed to the two-carat studs.

"Very lovely. It's not my affair whether Rick marries you or not. But Lindy *is* my business. Stay away from her."

"I'll show *you!*" Sharon spit out. "I'll have a ring to match the earrings."

"How nice. Now, if you'll excuse me, I have things to do," Vanessa said, holding open the library door.

"You're throwing me out? How dare you!"

"I'm simply asking you to leave, Sharon." She remained by the door, waiting for Sharon to walk out. She was so glad Lindy was at school. The girl shouldn't have to witness this scene.

Finally, Sharon walked into the hall. "Who is his lawyer? Since he got rid of that other one, I don't know who represents him."

"That's Rick's business, not mine."

"You're going to pay for your attitude, Vanessa Shaw!"

Vanessa said nothing. And when Sharon finally stormed down the hall and out the front door, Vanessa let out a big sigh.

Was Sharon really pregnant? It was possible the woman was scamming Rick. But if she was pregnant, what would Rick do? Vanessa was pretty sure he would not abandon his child. But would he marry Sharon?

With another sigh, Vanessa went to the kitchen,

where she knew Betty would have made her some lunch. Maybe she was just hungry—something was causing an emptiness in her stomach.

She reminded Betty and Peter, "No matter what that woman Sharon says, don't let her in the house again. Unless Rick is with her."

"Why would Rick have anything to do with her?" Betty asked.

"Because she says she's carrying his child."

Betty put a sandwich in front of Vanessa as she said, "I don't believe that."

Vanessa managed a small smile. She wished she didn't. But truthfully she didn't think even Sharon would be brazen enough to try faking a pregnancy. Surely Rick wouldn't marry her without proof. Then again, even if she was pregnant, the baby might not be Rick's. Sharon got around.

After trying to eat, Vanessa went to the library to call Jeff, on the off chance that Sharon had discovered he was Rick's attorney.

"Jeff, it's Vanessa. I thought I should give you a heads-up on a problem Rick is going to have."

"Going to have? Are you a fortune-teller now?"

Unfortunately not, she thought. If she were, she wouldn't be filled with uncertainty. She told Jeff about Sharon and her claims.

He was silent for a minute. Then he said, "Is it possible?"

"Whether it's possible or not would probably be

better answered by Rick. But I wouldn't trust her. She's wants to marry money, whatever it takes."

"Ah, one of those. Give me her last name and I'll start an investigation."

"Her name is Sharon Cresswell. She went to college with me and Carrie. I don't know what she does for a living, but she lives in Dallas."

"I'll find her. Thanks for letting me know. By the way, you haven't heard from Rick, have you?"

"No. He said he wouldn't be able to call us until his return, which should be in two weeks."

"Right. Okay, I'll talk to you later."

Just as Vanessa hung up the phone, she heard her mother come in. She walked out into the hall to greet her. "Hi, Mom, Danny. How are you doing? Did you have a good time at the birthday party?"

"Yes, 'Nessa! Look! I got a prize, too!" Danny held up a small water gun. "You put water in it and you can shoot water at people!"

"But only outside, and only if you are in a swimsuit, Danny. Remember?" Vivian prodded her son.

"Yes, Mommy. I 'member."

"Good. Go show Betty and Peter your prize."

Danny charged down the hall, calling for Betty and Peter.

Vanessa looked at her mother. "How are you, Mom? Danny has so much energy, I don't see how you keep up with him."

"I'm not sure I am anymore."

"Don't worry, Mom. It's not your age. It's being pregnant again. You need to take it easy. Come sit down and I'll get you something cool to drink."

When Vanessa got to the kitchen, Danny was still talking ninety miles a minute. "Danny, you need to go take your nap."

"Aw, 'Nessa, I'm a big boy. I don't need a nap."

"Yes, you do. Go upstairs and wash your hands. I'll come up and tuck you in."

After she'd settled both her brother and her mother upstairs, Vanessa curled up in one of the leather chairs in the library and attempted to spend the afternoon reading material both for her classes and for her doctorate research.

Unfortunately, her mind kept returning to the problem with Sharon that Rick was going to face. No matter how long she thought about it, she really didn't believe Sharon was pregnant with Rick's child, if she even was pregnant. Vanessa would guess that the idea hadn't occurred to Sharon until she realized she was going to lose Rick. After all, the woman was as far from the motherly type as you could get.

But if the baby wasn't Rick's, whose could it be? Vanessa knew Rick had said he only went out with Sharon occasionally. She must be dating someone else, too.

Vanessa hoped Will could figure it out. Maybe Jim or Carrie could find whom Sharon was dating. They were both good investigators. But Carrie was due soon. Will wouldn't send her out to do any investigations for a while.

Vanessa found herself smiling. More family. They would have babies all over the place. Probably David and Alex would start a family sometime soon, too.

How would Rick feel about a baby? Not the one Sharon was threatening him with, but any baby. If he married, would he want a family? He seemed to feel closer to Lindy now, but would he want children of his own? Vanessa thought he would, since he'd spent most of his youth as an only child, as she had. She remembered the other thing they had in common: that they'd both had a sibling enter the family after they were grown.

Life took such funny twists. Her father's death had freed her mother from a difficult marriage and her from a difficult parent and had brought them both Will. For Rick, his father's death had ended his family, until his stepmother's death had brought him and Lindy together again.

The phone rang and Vanessa, so deep in thought, jumped. Peter came from the kitchen.

"Rebecca is on the phone, Vanessa."

"Thank you, Peter." She crossed to the phone and greeted her sister. "How are you?"

"I'm fine, but I've talked to my husband. Are you sure *you're* fine?"

"He told you?"

"Well, he was concerned about you."

"I don't know why."

"Vanessa, you may be able to fool Vivian and Will, but not me! I saw the way you were looking at each other the other night when you came in after taking Lindy to the movies."

"We—we were pleased with how well the evening had gone."

"Exactly!"

"No, for Lindy!"

"Are you telling me he hasn't kissed you yet?" Rebecca asked.

"I— That's not a fair question!"

"But now I have my answer. So tell me. How's the romance developing?"

"We—we're just getting to know each other."

Rebecca chuckled. "Frankly, my dear, he seems more like the type to throw you over his shoulder and head for the cave."

"Rebecca!"

"Don't protest too much, Vanessa. I know that's not a politically correct statement, but it's still kind of romantic if he's the right guy."

"But I'm not sure he is."

"You're not going to let this Sharon person ruin things, are you?"

"No. I don't really believe her. But if Rick believes her, he might marry her."

"I hope not. She doesn't sound like the kind of

wife a man like Rick should have. Jeff says he's a really good guy."

"Yes, I think so, too."

"So why are you hesitating?" Rebecca asked.

"Because he's a million miles away in China. I can't even talk to him. How can I be sure when he's not here?" Vanessa could feel herself losing the tight control she'd been keeping on her emotions. She hadn't even admitted to herself that Rick might be the man for her.

"I—I really can't talk about this right now, 'Becca. I'm fine, but I—I need to go."

"Okay. Sorry if I upset you. You can call if you need to talk, though. I won't tease you anymore."

"That's what a sister is for, and I'm always grateful I have you and Rachel. Don't forget that."

"No, I won't."

Vanessa said goodbye and hung up the phone, then spent the next few minutes trying to rebuild her defenses.

VANESSA RETURNED to her studies after she picked up Lindy from school. In case Sharon went to the school to find her, Vanessa reminded Lindy that she was not to talk to Sharon.

"Why?"

"She's not the kind of person I want you to associate with."

"But she's a friend of Rick's."

"Yes, but she's not a nice person. And she doesn't always tell the truth. I don't want her to tell you things that will upset you, because they might not be true."

Lindy stared at Vanessa. Finally, she asked, "What did she say to you?"

Vanessa grinned. "You are one smart cookie, Lindy, but I'm not going to tell you. When Rick gets back, he can deal with Sharon. If what she says is true, Rick will tell you. Now go let Betty get you a snack. You know she doesn't think you can make it until dinner if you don't have a snack after school."

Lindy smiled. "I know. Isn't she wonderful?"

Once Lindy had gone to the kitchen, peace settled around Vanessa again for a while. Will got home an hour later, and came into the library when he saw Vanessa there.

"Hi, there. Is your mother napping?"

"Yes. I made sure she did. She was tired after taking Danny to his friend's birthday party."

"Thanks." He came over and sat down opposite her. "Jeff called me today."

"Oh?" she asked, trying to appear innocent.

"Yeah. He wants information on Sharon Cresswell. Carrie said the two of you know her."

"Yes, I do. I called Jeff today."

"About Sharon's claim? She's the one who told you?"

"Yes. Jeff asked if I believe her. I don't want to, but Rick has dated Sharon off and on. So I guess it's a possibility. He stopped dating her when I told him she wasn't a good person for Lindy to be around."

"Yeah, that's what I thought. Jim's going to see what he can find out."

"Why not Alex?"

"Because men will talk more freely with another man than they will with a woman."

Vanessa nodded.

"What about Lindy?"

"I told her not to talk to Sharon. Of course, that made her curious. I told her that I didn't want her to be upset by anything Sharon said, because she's been known to lie."

Will patted her hand. "We'll see what we can find out."

"If there's anything I can do, please let me know."

"You're already helping by making sure your mother gets her rest. I worry about her, you know."

"I know, Will. But I'll help you keep an eye on her. Right now she just tires easily. But that's normal, no matter what age you are. 'Becca will tell you. Or Rachel. They've both gone through it."

"Yeah, I know. I remember when she was pregnant with Danny."

Having heard Will's voice, Betty came in. "Would you like an iced tea?"

"No, I'm fine, Betty. Is Danny up yet?"

"Sure thing. He's in the kitchen with Peter. You ready for him?"

Vanessa couldn't hold back a grin at Betty's choice of words. Will nodded and seconds after Betty called Danny, the boy came through the door like a tornado. He leaped into his dad's arms, talking as fast as he could, repeating all the information about his water gun.

"I'm going up to see how Lindy is doing with her homework," Vanessa told Will. "I'll check on Mom, too."

She found Lindy on the phone talking to a new friend. That was a good sign. She was beginning to act like a normal teenager.

"Excuse me, Lindy, but did you finish your homework?"

Lindy covered the phone receiver. "Yes, but I'd like you to check my French. The grammar is a little complicated and I'm not sure I got it right."

She pointed to some papers on her desk.

Vanessa reached over and found the French assignment, took it to her room next door and ran over it quickly, finding a couple of mistakes. She returned to Lindy's room and, after Lindy hung up, Vanessa explained the errors.

"Now I'm going to check on Mom. Dinner will be served in about fifteen minutes."

"Okay. I'll go down and see if I can help Betty."

"Thanks, Lindy."

When she knocked on her mother's door, she didn't hear any movement. Opening the door, she found her mother still asleep, which meant that she'd slept for more than three hours.

"Mom? It's time to get up for supper."

"Oh my. I've slept that long?"

Vanessa nodded. "Are you feeling all right?"

"Yes, but the birthday party was draining."

"Next time, make Will go."

Vivian grinned. "Yeah, then he can get his ear chewed off about that silly water gun."

"He already is." Vanessa cocked her head toward the stairs.

Her mother stood up. "In that case, let's go rescue my man."

WAITING FOR RICK'S RETURN was more draining than Vanessa had expected. At least Jeff was taking care of the problem Sharon had revealed. Vanessa didn't want to discuss the possibility of Rick's child, though she did have some thoughts about him and his father choosing the same type of woman.

The day he was expected back in the States, she found herself on edge. When the phone rang that afternoon she jumped. She grabbed the receiver at once. "Hello?"

"Hi, Vanessa. It's Rick. How are you?"

The sound of his voice warmed her. She resisted the urge to sigh and instead adopted a neutral tone. "Fine. Are you in D.C.?"

"Yeah. We got in about an hour ago. It looks like

I'll have to stay here for a couple more days, but I wanted to be sure you and Lindy were fine."

"We're both doing well."

"Did you miss me?" he asked, his voice dropping to a personal level that sent shivers through her body.

"Lindy talked about you constantly."

"That wasn't my question. Did *you* miss me?"

No way would she answer that. "Rick, I think you need to talk to Jeff."

After a moment of silence, he asked, "Why?"

"Something has come up. Something personal."

"And it's made you back off, right?"

She feigned innocence. "I don't know what you're talking about."

"You don't remember kissing me goodbye?"

Vanessa said hastily, "*You* kissed *me!*"

She could hear the grin in his answer.

"Good. You do remember. Now, what's the problem?"

Vanessa let out a sigh. She hadn't wanted to be the one to tell him. But he'd pushed her into a corner and she had nowhere to escape. "Sharon came to see me."

"Why?" he asked.

"She needed to find you. She—" How else could she say it? There was only one way. "She said she was pregnant."

More silence. Then Rick asked, "What does that have to do with me?"

"She said it's yours."

"No!"

Vanessa didn't say anything.

"You believed her?"

"I don't know, Rick! Did you— Were you intimate with her?"

He huffed into the phone. "A time or two, yeah. But I always used protection."

"Accidents happen. That's why I contacted Jeff."

"You should've thrown her out on her ear!"

"I felt like doing that. But what if she is carrying your child?"

Rick said, "I'll call Jeff."

"Okay. I'll tell Lindy you're back and that you called."

"Yeah, thanks." And he hung up the phone.

Vanessa sat there, staring at the wall, a tear drifting down her cheek. When she realized she was crying, she silently gave herself a stern lecture. She had nothing to cry about. She would have her doctorate in six months. She had Lindy in her life. She had her wonderful family. She had more than most people.

But something that had only been a shimmering idea in the air, not yet real, but possible, had died.

"I CAN'T BE THE FATHER of her baby!" Rick was nearly shouting into the phone at his attorney. "I had sex with her twice but I used a condom both times. This has to be bogus."

"Rick, calm down." Jeff Jacobs spoke evenly, his

voice reassuring, making Rick stop pacing inside his D.C. hotel room. "I'm glad to hear that you used protection. I'm sure Will's firm will turn up something. In the meantime, you must refuse to pay for anything until after the birth of the child, when you and the baby can be tested." He paused, then said, "Unless you want to marry the woman, of course."

Rick felt his blood pressure spike. "No!"

"Then I'll proceed with what I've set in motion."

"Good."

"You don't know anything that will help me, do you? Can you tell me the names of anyone else she's dated?"

"No."

"How did the two of you meet?"

"We met at a party given by the S.M.U. alumni association." He sat down at the foot of the bed. "Come to think of it, I wonder why Vanessa didn't attend."

"I don't know. Did someone introduce you?"

"Obviously you've never met Sharon. My guess would be someone pointed me out to her. She waltzed up and introduced herself. Before she left, she stuck her phone number in my pocket."

"What made you call her?"

"I hadn't spent a lot of time on my social life and I needed a date for a function I had to attend. So two weeks later, I called her. She accepted and she looked great. She was a little clingy, but not too bad. I didn't even think about her for about a month, until I needed a date for a business dinner. I called her and she accepted at once. There was no complaint about me not having called her for so long. That charmed me. We had sex that night." He hated to admit it.

"And what was the date?"

"I'll have to look in my calendar." From his briefcase he pulled out a small date book that he always carried with him. "Here it is. The dinner was three months ago on June third."

"I don't think she would've waited so long to claim a pregnancy. When was the next time?"

"About six weeks ago. She started calling me. That should've been a sign to me, but I didn't pay attention. She went to a dinner with me and begged me to make love to her again. I did so reluctantly. But it was my fault."

"Okay, that would be the date. And you're sure you used protection?"

"A condom. Definitely."

"All right, we'll work something out. When you talk to her, give her my name and number and tell her to come talk to me. Don't discuss anything with her yourself."

"Gladly. I don't want to talk to her. I don't want to see her."

"I can't guarantee you won't have to see or talk to her, but we'll get you through this, Rick, I promise."

"Thanks."

"When will you get back here?"

"They told us they'd need at least two days. I'm hoping to fly in Wednesday evening, but it may be Thursday."

"Well, give me a call after you give my information to Sharon."

"You're sure you want me to have her call you?"

"Isn't that what you hired me for?"

"Yeah, it is. But my last lawyer wasn't so eager to be helpful."

"I believe in earning my money," Jeff said with a laugh.

"Thanks. I appreciate that."

"All right, I'll talk to you in a couple of days."

They said goodbye and hung up.

That was one good thing: Jeff was a great lawyer who did his job well. Lindy was another good thing. And best of all was Vanessa.

But the hope he'd had of a future with her had to be put on hold until he cleared up past mistakes.

He just hoped that would happen soon.

Chapter Eleven

Rick got back to Dallas on Thursday afternoon, and went to his office first. His secretary had a big stack of messages, five of which were from Sharon.

With a sigh, he grabbed the phone and dialed her number, knowing she wouldn't be home from work. When the answering machine picked up, he left her a message telling her to contact his lawyer and giving her the necessary information.

While he hoped that meant he wouldn't have to talk to her, he knew better. She'd be calling him this evening, as soon as she got that message.

But she'd have to wait. He had other plans for tonight.

He called the Greenfields and spoke to Vivian. "I'm back from China and wondered if this evening would be convenient for me to visit with Lindy."

"I'm sure it would," Vivian said. "Why don't you come for dinner? We'll eat at seven. We'd all love to hear about your adventures."

"Thank you, Vivian. I'd love to."

He hung up the phone, a smile on his face. He should feel bad. He had known Vivian would invite him. But he wanted—needed—to see Lindy and Vanessa.

After he went home and unpacked and gave a gift to Mrs. Abby, he hurried to the Greenfields'. When Peter opened the door, he gave him a present for him and Betty, too, much to Peter's surprise.

When he reached the morning room where Will and Vivian were playing with Danny, he set a big box on the coffee table.

"What's that?" Vivian asked.

"A present I brought back for you and Will."

"Oh my!" Vivian exclaimed, eagerly reaching for it.

"Be careful! It's very easily broken," Rick warned.

Vivian sat up even straighter. "Don't tell me it's eggshell porcelain? Oh, Rick, how wonderful! I've always wanted one of those."

"What is it?" Will asked.

"Eggshell porcelain is so thin, you can almost see through it."

"So it's white and thin?" Will asked, clearly not getting the appeal.

"Not white. They're hand-painted in beautiful colors."

"Honey, if you wanted one, why didn't you go buy one?"

"Because they stopped shipping them. They would break in transit because they're so fragile."

Will slowly opened the box, which was packed in foam. He lifted off the top piece of foam and found other packing, then tissue paper. In all, it took several minutes to uncover a richly painted porcelain bowl.

Vivian drew a deep breath and released it with an "Ah!"

"Man, it's impressive," Will said. "Can I take it out of the box?"

Vivian carefully cleared off the coffee table where he could set the bowl. "Rick, it's gorgeous. Thank you."

"I'm glad you like it. I wanted to show my gratitude for keeping Lindy."

"We hardly know she's here. She's so well behaved. And she loves playing with Danny. He's used to having time with her."

"I'm glad she's doing so well here."

"Are you talking about me?" Lindy asked as she entered the room and ran toward her brother.

"Yeah, but we're only saying good things," Rick promised, giving his sister a bear hug.

"Oh, that's pretty," Lindy said, her attention going to the bowl.

"Isn't it?" Vivian said with a big smile. "Your brother brought it back from China for us."

"To thank them for putting up with you," Rick teased.

Lindy grinned to show she knew he was joking. "So what did you bring me?" she asked.

"You? I was supposed to bring *you* something?"

"Rick!" Lindy protested.

He smiled and handed her a box. "Go put this on and come show us."

She hurriedly opened it and found a beautiful Chinese dress in lavender silk. "Oh, that's wonderful. Do you think it will fit me?"

"It should, unless you've been eating too much lately."

She grinned. "I'll be right back!"

She raced out of the room, and Rick turned to the other two. "She's beginning to sound like a real teenager."

Will said, "Thank goodness she has her own cell phone, because she's on it a lot. But not until she's finished her homework each afternoon."

"I'm glad to hear it—"

Suddenly, he knew Vanessa had entered the room, though she hadn't made any noise. It was her light floral fragrance that alerted him. He turned slowly around.

"Hello, Vanessa."

"Hello, Rick. How was China?"

"It was interesting."

Vanessa must have caught sight of the bowl on her mother's coffee table. "Mom, what's that?"

"It's an eggshell porcelain bowl from China. Isn't it marvelous?"

"Yes, it is. Did you bring that back for Lindy?" she asked Rick.

"No, that's for your mom and dad to thank them for taking care of Lindy."

"I thought I was the one taking care of Lindy," Vanessa asked, raising her eyebrows.

Rick smiled, but he said, "I need to speak to you in the library. Would now be a good time?"

"I—I guess so," she said. With a quick look at Will and Vivian, she turned and walked out of the room, Rick following her.

Once they were in the library, the door closed behind them, Rick moved in close to Vanessa. She took a step back.

"Rick, I don't think we should—"

"So you believe Sharon?"

"I don't, really, but I think things should be cleared up before—before we go any further."

Rick wanted to use every bad word he'd heard in his life. He'd been waiting to hold Vanessa again. To kiss her. To tell her he couldn't live without her…

He ground his teeth together, being careful not to move an inch, because if he did, he might lose control.

Finally, he reached into his inside coat pocket and pulled out a long, slender box. "I did bring you a gift from China."

His words seemed to break the tension. She smiled a little nervously and said, "You didn't need to do that."

"I think I did. Here, open it."

He'd chosen her gift carefully. A rare jade set in a platinum bracelet.

Vanessa stared at it. "You shouldn't have, Rick! Charcoal jade is horribly expensive."

"I thought it would look beautiful on you, especially with that black cocktail dress you wore when we went to NaNa's together."

"You're right, it will look beautiful with that dress."

"Here, let me put it on your wrist…to see if it fits." It would also give him a chance to touch her.

She took the bracelet from the box and handed it to him. He took it in one hand and caught her wrist in the other, feeling the shivers that coursed through her. He wanted to forget the bracelet, pull her into his arms and kiss her senseless. "Vanessa—"

"No! Just—just fasten the bracelet for me, Rick. That's all."

"Fine!" he said curtly. She must be made of iron, he thought with a grimace, but he knew better than that.

He fastened the bracelet around her wrist, her skin warm under his touch. Then, before she could pull it away, he bent over and kissed her wrist.

VANESSA PULLED HER WRIST back as she stepped away from Rick's reach. "Was the bracelet the reason we came to the library? Because you could've—"

"No. I promised my housekeeper I'd talk to you about letting Lindy come to live at my house. Mrs.

Abby wants to take care of Lindy. She'd be there when I went out of town, and I thought that might work out."

"You promised me a year, Rick. Lindy has made wonderful progress, but she still has a long way to go. Please don't even think of taking her away from me yet."

"Okay, okay, honey. If you think she needs to stay here longer, I'll leave her here. You've been right about everything else you've said about Lindy."

Vanessa composed herself. "Thank you, Rick. Are you ready to join the others now?"

"Yeah, if you're not going to allow me to kiss you."

"I don't think—"

"Yeah, you've said that, but I don't think one kiss would cause a train wreck."

Vanessa closed her eyes. But he was still there when she opened them—and she couldn't say no. "Okay. One kiss."

Almost before she finished speaking, she was wrapped in Rick's strong arms, his lips seeking hers in a kiss that was, at the same time, too long and too short. When he finally released her, they were both breathing like they'd run a marathon.

"That—that was definitely some kiss," she said. Then she composed herself. "Let's go join the others." She didn't wait for his compliance. She needed to get away from him before she forgot everything she'd decided before he got home.

THEY HAD JUST REJOINED Will and Vivian when Lindy came back into the room, wearing her lavender dress.

"Chinese women certainly can't take big steps in a dress like this," she said.

"Oh, Lindy, you look beautiful," Vanessa sighed.

"You do, Lindy," Rick said. "And here's something to go with it." He pulled out a second long box and opened it, holding out the box so Lindy could see the dainty bracelet made of jade and gold.

Vanessa smiled at Lindy. "Rick got me a bracelet, too."

"Let me see, dear," Vivian said from the sofa.

Vanessa crossed over to Vivian and extended her arm to her mother.

"You have lovely taste, Rick," Vivian said.

"Thank you. I think so—in other things too, besides jewelry." He smiled at the two young ladies sporting his gifts.

Peter appeared at the door. "Dinner is served, Miss Vivian."

"Thank you, Peter. Look at the eggshell porcelain bowl Rick brought us from China. It's very fragile."

"He brought us a jade statue of Buddha. It brings you good luck if you rub its tummy." Peter beamed at Rick.

"I'll be sure to rub his tummy before I take my next test," Lindy said.

"You'd better be *studying* for those tests, young lady," Rick said sternly.

"Oh, I do. You can ask Vanessa," Lindy said hurriedly, clearly wanting Rick to be proud of her.

"Okay, I believe it." He hugged Lindy again, his gaze meeting Vanessa's over Lindy's head.

But Vanessa abruptly turned and walked toward the dining room.

AFTER DINNER they all listened to Rick's stories about his trip to China. At ten, however, Vanessa reminded Lindy it was her bedtime.

"Can't I stay up late tonight?"

"No, sweetie, it's a school night. You'll see Rick again soon."

"Okay," Lindy agreed, but they all heard the irritation in her voice.

She kissed everyone good-night and went upstairs.

Rick looked at Vanessa. "Is she giving you trouble?"

"No, not at all."

"She didn't sound pleased that you sent her up to bed."

Before Vanessa could respond, Vivian laughed. "Vanessa says that's a good sign."

"What do you mean? Doesn't it mean she'd like to rebel?"

"Of course it does," Vanessa replied. "But a child who fears for her place in the family would never dare complain. That's how we know Lindy is progressing."

"So she's back to normal?"

"No, not yet. She's just getting used to us and testing her limits a little. We have a ways to go."

Rick nodded thoughtfully, remembering what she'd said in the library.

Will stood and pulled Vivian to her feet. "Pregnant moms need to go to bed early—they need their sleep." He turned to Rick. "You're lucky she didn't fall asleep during your description of your trip to China."

Vivian tapped her husband on his arm. "Nonsense, Rick, we enjoyed this evening very much. I hope you'll join us again soon."

Rick nodded. "Thank you, Vivian." He bid them both good-night as they left the room.

Rick remained standing. Now he looked at Vanessa, still seated on the sofa. "May I join you?"

"No, Rick, I don't think we can—I think you should go home. I'm sure you're tired, as long a day as you've had."

"Without a goodbye kiss?"

"Just go, please!"

"When will I get to see you again?"

"Probably tomorrow. I'm sure Will will want to talk to you. About Sharon."

There it was again. The insurmountable barrier between them.

THE NEXT DAY when Vanessa got home from school, she found Will and Rick in the library. They both invited her in.

"Don't you want to talk without me? I mean, about Sharon?"

"Actually, I thought maybe you could contribute to what we know. That's why I asked Rick to meet me here," Will said.

Vanessa stared at Rick, and he nodded.

"Of course I'll be glad to join you, but I don't know how much I can add," she said.

Once they were all seated in the library, Will asked Vanessa if she had any knowledge of Sharon dating other men.

"We're not that close, Will. I mean, I'd see her out occasionally, but— Well, there was one guy she was with more often than anyone else. I'd forgotten about him."

"Who was he?" Will asked.

"I remember her introducing him as Larry."

"No last name?"

Vanessa shook her head.

"When was the last time you saw them together?"

"The end of the school year. I went to the eighth grade graduation at a local school. A patient of mine was graduating. I saw Sharon and Larry at the reception."

"Was he there as a part of the family?"

Vanessa shook her head. "No, I think— No, he was introduced as the child's math teacher!"

"Good girl," Will said. "This will help Jim a lot."

"She never mentioned this man to me," Rick interjected.

"Of course she didn't, Rick. That wouldn't serve her purpose." Vanessa gave him a superior look.

"What purpose?"

"To get as much money out of you as she can," she said.

"How do you know that's what she's doing?"

"Rick, she's been trying to get rich the old-fashioned way, by marrying a rich man, ever since I met her. You're just one of several."

"I should've known she was being too accommodating."

Will gave him a sympathetic smile. "We men have trouble understanding women, Rick. It happens."

"Not to me. It's never happened to me until now."

"With this information, I think Jim will be able to track down this Larry. If they are still dating, I think he'll be shocked by Sharon's behavior. And he may be able to give us some leverage for a discussion with her."

"What can I do to help?" Rick asked.

"Have you talked to her yet?"

"I left a message on her answering machine giving her the name of my lawyer and asking her to talk to him. She'd left a number of messages at my office and at home."

"Okay, the first thing you can do is avoid talking

to her. But if you are forced into it, record the conversation."

"Why?"

"She may claim you said all kinds of things. If we have a recording, she'll have no place to go."

"Good thinking. Okay, I'll get a mini-recorder and keep it with me at all times."

"Again, if you have to talk to her, try to get her to give you the name of her doctor."

"But medical records are private."

"I know. But you never know what you'll find out if you push hard enough."

"I don't want you to break any laws, Will."

"We don't do that, Rick, I promise."

"Okay. If this child is mine, I'll pay, of course, but—"

"Don't say that to Sharon. Just tell her to get in touch with your lawyer. He'll explain the terms to her."

"I haven't actually talked to Jeff since I got back home. I had other things on my mind last night."

Will picked up the phone on the desk and dialed Jeff's number. Then he punched a button that switched it to speakerphone. When Jeff answered, he identified himself and told Jeff he had the speaker on. "Rick and Vanessa are in here with me. Rick said he didn't get a chance to talk to you about Sharon last night. But he wanted you to know he's left a message for her to call you."

"I haven't talked to her yet," Jeff replied. "Here's

what I propose we tell her, Rick. You can let me know if you disagree with it. Since there is some doubt about your having fathered the baby, I suggest we tell her you will pay any doctor bills if she gives the doctor permission to reveal her medical information to you. Any additional payout will not occur until after the birth of the child, when DNA testing can be done safely."

"Do you think we have to be that difficult? If she's carrying my child, I want her to have what she needs," Rick said.

"That's what she's counting on. If we remain firm, she may realize her tactics are useless, unless the baby really is yours. Just don't deal with her. She'll play on your sympathy. Keep saying over and over, 'Call my lawyer.'"

"Okay, I'll do what you say. And thanks."

After Will thanked him, too, he disconnected the call. "Feel better?" he asked Rick.

"Yeah, but I'd like this resolved sooner rather than later."

"You're not the only one," Vanessa muttered.

When both men stared at her, Vanessa asked, "I didn't say that out loud, did I?" She could feel her cheeks start to heat up and she scrambled for an excuse. "I—I meant because of Lindy, of course. I feel sure Sharon will try to get to her, if she can't get to you."

"Why would she do that?" Rick asked.

"Because Lindy would be excited that you were having a baby and she wouldn't understand the motives of someone like Sharon."

"That's true," Rick said. "But you'll keep her away from Sharon, won't you?"

"Of course."

That settled, Will stood up and said, "I guess that's all we need to talk about. I'll give Jim the information and he'll see what he can find out."

Rick stood and shook Will's hand. "I appreciate all you're doing."

Will grinned. "Don't worry. We'll bill you." Then he added, as he headed for the door, "Thanks, Vanessa."

"But—" Vanessa began, then stopped. There was no point in trying to persuade Will to stay. He was already gone.

"Well," she said, stopping to clear her throat. "I'm sure you have things to do. I don't want to hold you up." She stood and looked toward the door.

"Not so fast." Rick stepped closer. "I want you to know that I have no intention of marrying Sharon whether she's carrying my child or not. But I truly believe she's not."

"I hope you're right," Vanessa said softly, looking away.

"I just want to tell you not to go falling for some other guy in the meantime."

"I don't know what you're talking about," Vanessa protested.

"Yes, you do. There was something between us from the beginning. So, I'll be back. You be ready."

"I don't respond to threats."

He moved closer and dropped a quick kiss on her lips. "It's not a threat. It's a promise."

Chapter Twelve

Things seemed normal in the Greenfield household for several days. Rick wasn't mentioned by anyone. But that didn't mean that Vanessa didn't think about him. In fact, thoughts of Rick were driving her crazy.

She was worried about his future. If he was wrong and Sharon *was* carrying his baby, he might actually marry her, and she, Vanessa, couldn't blame him. In fact, she might even insist. A child left to Sharon's care would only suffer.

Vanessa shook her head to clear her thoughts.

"Is something wrong, dear?" Vivian asked.

"Oh, no, I, um, was thinking about something that happened at the university this morning."

"Oh. I keep thinking we'll hear more about Rick's situation. I do worry about that."

"He'll be fine, Mom. Don't fret about him."

"But he's such a nice man. And he's already been victimized by his stepmother as much as Lindy was. Sharon seems to be the same kind of woman."

"I know. I'm thinking about doing a study of how some men attract the same kind of woman from father to son. It's interesting, isn't it?"

"I doubt Rick finds it interesting. You know, Vanessa, sometimes I fear that you try to keep certain people distant by studying them as if they were bugs under a microscope."

"Mom!"

"Well, dear, it's very difficult when you study people and their reactions all day long, not to do so in your personal life."

"I don't— I'll try not to do that, Mom."

Betty appeared in the doorway. "That lady is outside and Lindy is due to arrive home any minute."

Lindy had begged and pleaded to carpool home from school with her best friend. Today the friend's mother would bring them home.

"Oh dear, I've got to go chase her off," Vanessa said. She grabbed her mother's cell phone from a lamp table. "I'm going to borrow this, Mom."

"Of course," Vivian said. She followed more slowly as Vanessa raced out the door.

Vanessa reached the front door in time to watch Lindy arrive. She sped down the sidewalk to the girl. Out of the corner of her eye, she saw Sharon get out of her car.

"Just drive away, Sharon, or I'm calling the police," Vanessa called as she opened the car door for Lindy to get out.

"I don't have to do that. I'm not breaking any laws," Sharon protested. "I just want to speak to my baby's aunt."

"What's she saying?" Lindy asked, turning to stare at Sharon.

"Just ignore her," Vanessa told Lindy. Then she said to Sharon again, "I'm calling the police, Sharon, and telling them you're trespassing."

"I'm on a public street, I'll have you know!" Sharon said, standing in the street behind her car.

Vanessa pulled Lindy toward the door where Betty and Vivian stood waiting.

"Why does she want to talk to me?" Lindy asked Vanessa.

"She's lying and hopes to get sympathy from you to use against your brother."

Suddenly Lindy stopped resisting and hurried to the front door.

Obviously realizing she wasn't going to get any attention from the street, Sharon started running up the walk. She reached the front door just after Lindy and Vanessa entered and closed it. She immediately rang the doorbell.

Vanessa, having sent Lindy into the morning room with Vivian, opened the door, Peter beside her. "Yes?"

"I want to talk to Lindy!"

Vanessa studied the woman. "I'm afraid she's not available."

"I just saw her go in. I know she's in there."

Vanessa didn't bother to argue. "So?"

"I want to talk to her."

"No."

"Fine! But I'll find a way!"

"You can try. But then I'll report you for harassment."

"We're going to be kin. You can't keep me out."

"Goodbye," Vanessa said firmly, and slammed the door in Sharon's face.

"That woman is trouble," Peter muttered.

"Yes, she is. Don't let her in, no matter who she asks to talk to or what she says she wants."

"I won't."

When Vanessa reached the morning room, she found her mother lying back on the sofa with her eyes closed and Lindy pacing the floor. On the coffee table was a tray with iced tea and cookies, no doubt courtesy of Betty.

When she saw Vanessa, Lindy demanded to know what Sharon wanted to tell her.

"I think your best protection is to explain the situation to her, dear," Vivian said, sitting up and opening her eyes.

"Are you feeling all right, Mom?" Vanessa asked.

"Yes, I'm fine, but I didn't want to answer any of Lindy's questions."

"I wish *I* didn't have to," Vanessa said with a sigh.

"Fine! I'll ask Rick," exclaimed Lindy.

Vanessa ducked her head to hide her smile at Lindy's stubbornness.

"No, sit down, sweetie. I'll explain."

Lindy sat on the sofa and Vanessa joined her. "First, I have to ask if you know where babies come from." Vanessa watched Lindy closely.

Though her cheeks flushed, Lindy tried to appear blasé. She put down the cookie she was eating. "Yes, of course."

"I hope you know that it can happen when a man and a woman have sex. You'll notice I didn't say anything about love. Men and women have physical urges that they sometimes give in to even if they aren't in love. Your brother has occasionally indulged in sex. While he contends that when he did so with Sharon, he used condoms, she says she's pregnant."

"Pregnant? You mean Rick's going to have a baby?" Lindy asked, excitement in her voice.

"We don't know if it's his, honey. Sharon has been known to lie."

"Why would she do that?"

"Some women will do whatever it takes to get a man with a lot of money to marry them."

Lindy frowned. "But if she's pregnant, doesn't that mean— Whose baby is it?"

"We're not sure. But we don't think she should try to use you against your brother."

"I don't think she should, either."

"So I hope you'll wait until Rick knows. When he does, he'll tell you."

Lindy nodded. Vanessa then turned to Vivian. "I hope I didn't upset you," she said tentatively.

"No, dear, you didn't. Besides, you shared your cookies with me. I'll forgive anything for chocolate chips like these."

"Mom, you know Betty would fix anything you wanted."

"I know, dear, but I wanted Lindy to feel better."

Vanessa shared a smile with her mother.

Peter came to the door. "Vanessa, Mr. Rick's on the phone."

"Oh, all right. I'll get it in the library. I didn't even hear the phone ring. Lindy, you should get busy on your homework. I'll come check with you when I get off the phone."

"Okay. Tell Rick I said hi."

Vanessa ignored the wistful tone in Lindy's voice as she shooed the young girl upstairs. Then she went to the library and took a moment to compose herself before she picked up the phone.

"Hello, Rick."

"Hi, Vanessa. I called to be sure everything was okay there. About Sharon, I mean."

"Are you psychic?" she asked in surprise.

"No, but she talked to Jeff today, and she threatened to talk to Lindy."

Vanessa sighed. "She tried." She told Rick about the confrontation with Sharon.

"Good," he said when she was done. "That will take care of it, I'm sure."

"I'm not. I agreed with Mom, the best defense is offense. We thought it better to tell Lindy why Sharon wanted to talk to her."

"You did *what?*" Rick asked, his voice going up several decibels.

"She said if we didn't tell her what was going on, she'd ask you," Vanessa said gently, and waited for a response.

Silence.

"Did *you* want to explain everything to Lindy?" she prompted.

"No," he answered quickly. Then he added, "But I don't want her to hate me, either."

"She doesn't, Rick, I promise. And, uh, she'll need more information before she starts dating, but—"

"Dating? She's not—"

"No, she's not ready for dating. Maybe next year."

"But she'll only be sixteen!"

Patiently, Vanessa said, "I know that, Rick. Most girls start dating at sixteen."

"Absolutely not!"

"Rick, that's why she's living with me. I can handle a talk about sex without overreacting. I can understand her need to fit in with her friends…to some degree."

"Okay, I won't argue with you. At least not right now. I, uh, had another reason for calling."

"You mean they've already found out about the baby?" she asked.

"No."

"Then what—"

"I need you to go out with me tomorrow night."

"No! Absolutely not!"

"But, Vanessa, you are the *only* one I can ask."

"Why?"

"Because you know what's going on in my life, for one reason."

"Do you have other reasons?"

"Yes. I haven't met another woman to fill in."

"Can't you hire someone? I mean, aren't there real escort services you can call?"

"Not for a business function. There are only places to rent a prostitute."

"I'm sure you're wrong."

"I may be, but I need someone I can trust. Someone who knows how to behave in public, carry on intelligent conversations. You were great with the Williamses."

"Am I supposed to say thank you?"

"No, just say you'll go."

"What are you going to?"

"They've asked me to speak to a group of elite businesspeople in town, and they're all coming with spouses."

Vanessa let out a heavy sigh. "Fine. One last time."

"I can't promise—"

"Surely once you clear up the problem with Sharon you can meet someone new."

"Why would I want to?"

"What?"

"I told you I want you. I'll court you," he added, as if he anticipated a protest.

"I—I don't know what—"

"We'll talk about it later. I'll pick you up at six forty-five tomorrow night. And it's cocktail dress. Thanks for agreeing." And he hung up.

"Smart man," Vanessa muttered.

Then she picked up the phone again and dialed the number for Greenfield and Associates. When Carrie answered, she asked for Will, who soon came on the line.

"Hello?"

"Will, it's Vanessa. I know I shouldn't ask, but what's happening on Rick's problem?"

Will took a deep breath. "You're right. You shouldn't ask."

"But I helped provide information, didn't I? Can't you at least tell me if you've found the man Sharon was dating?"

"We know who he is, but he's away on vacation."

"But school has already started!"

"We know. Seems his sister is getting married on

Saturday night. He'll come back on Sunday and be in school next Monday."

Vanessa groaned in frustration.

"What happened that made you call me?" Will asked.

"Oh, Sharon tried to talk to Lindy…and Rick needs me to go to a dinner with him tomorrow night."

"Ah. Well, I do think he's stuck right now."

"Yes, so he explained."

"Do you really not want to go out with him?"

"No, it's just…I don't mind, but it would be better if he didn't have this pregnancy claim hanging over his head."

"I agree, honey, but I think this will soon be re-solved."

"Thanks, Will."

"And, Vanessa?"

"Yes?"

"Anything *Rick* wants to tell you is fine."

"Right. Thank you."

She hung up the phone and wandered back into the morning room.

"Was Lindy finishing her homework?"

Vanessa looked at her mother in surprise. "I don't know. I haven't checked on her."

"You haven't? What have you been doing?"

Vanessa told her mother about Rick's call, then her conversation with Will.

Vivian gave her a sympathetic smile but said, "You shouldn't have asked Will for information."

"I know. He told me. It's just… Rick needs me to go to another dinner with him tomorrow night."

"I see."

"I just wanted to know if they had found out any more about Sharon's pregnancy. If it's his, I think he should either sue for custody or marry Sharon. Can you imagine the damage Sharon could do to that child?"

"That's Rick's decision, dear. After he makes his decision, you also may have a decision to make."

Vanessa collapsed on the sofa beside her mother. "Mom, I don't know what to do!"

Vivian smiled. "I can't tell you how long I've waited for you to say those words."

Vanessa turned to stare at her mother. "Why?"

"Because a mother wants to feel needed. You were such a determined child. It wasn't often that you asked for any guidance."

Vanessa struggled to hold back the tears. "I always needed you, Mom. Always. But can you help me now?"

"I have only one piece of advice, dear. Follow your heart. I don't believe it will steer you wrong."

WHEN RICK CAME TO THE HOUSE a few minutes early to speak with Lindy, he was a little surprised that she rushed into his arms for a hug as usual.

"You're not unhappy with me?" he asked.

"No, Vanessa explained everything."

"Okay," Rick said, drawing out the word while he thought about what Vanessa must have said.

"She explained that Sharon wanted to use me against you. I'll never go against you, Rick. You took me back after Mom died, and I'll always be on your side."

Rick had to swallow back a lump in his throat. "That must've been some explanation, kid. I'm the one who didn't take care of you for nine years. You're being too generous."

"I'm just a little worried about what kind of mother Sharon will be. I mean, if it's really your baby."

"Yeah, I know."

"What will you do if it is?"

"I don't know, honey. I'll probably pay Sharon a lot of money to give the baby to me. Money is what she wants."

Lindy stood there looking at Rick. "I'm glad we have a lot of money. You can use some of mine, too."

He was so moved, he hugged her again. "I don't deserve your generosity. But I promise I'll always be on your side, too, no matter what."

"Can anyone get in on this hug fest?" Vivian asked as she and Will entered the room.

"Of course!" Lindy said at once and threw her arms around Vivian.

Just then, Vanessa entered, and Rick immediately held out his arms. "Need a hug?"

Chapter Thirteen

"No! I don't need a hug. What's going on?"

"I hugged Lindy because she offered some of her money to get rid of Sharon. Your mom and Will came in and wanted to have hugs, too. Lindy took care of them, so I figured I should do my part." Rick shot her a grin.

Vanessa stepped back. "I don't think that's necessary. Are you ready to go?"

Rick looked her up and down, admiration in his gaze. "You bet. And it's obvious you are." He'd also noted she was wearing the bracelet he'd brought her from China. Since she was wearing a silver and black cocktail dress, it was a perfect match.

"We'll see you later," Vanessa told Will. "I'm not sure how late we'll be."

"Don't worry about it," Will assured her. "We'll keep an eye on Lindy."

Vanessa leaned forward and kissed Lindy's cheek, then her mother's.

Rick escorted Vanessa to his car. "You look wonderful tonight."

"Thank you," she said as she slid into the passenger seat.

When he got in beside her, she asked, "Where are we going?"

He named The Mansion, a world-famous hotel on the outskirts of Highland Park.

"Very nice," she murmured.

"Yes, it is. The guests are almost as impressive, too. All the leaders in business and education in the Dallas area will be there."

"Education?"

"Of course. They teach the next generation of businesspeople. We need to be sure they're on the cutting edge."

"So it'll be only business professors?"

"I believe it was open to any professors. Why? What are you worried about?"

"Nothing," Vanessa lied. If her supervisory professor Dr. Cavanaugh was there, she didn't think he'd be pleased to discover anything that hinted of romance between her and Lindy's brother.

The man had the power to deny her completion of her doctorate in psychology if he thought she'd broken the rules set down for psychologists and their patients. She'd just have to hope Dr. Cavanaugh had somewhere else to be tonight.

When they reached the hotel, Rick pulled in for

valet parking. His door was immediately opened, as was Vanessa's. The valet helped her out of the car and Rick hurried around to take her hand.

Vanessa resisted, but he insisted on holding her hand. "We're not dining in the restaurant," he murmured. "I'll show you where to go."

She left her hand in his. It wouldn't look right to struggle in the hotel.

He led her down the hall into the ballroom, a massive elegantly decorated room where they were immediately met by two men Vanessa didn't know.

Rick introduced her to them. One of the men claimed to have known her father. She greeted the man, but reserved an opinion of anyone who felt he had been close to her father. She hadn't been close to him, and she hadn't liked the way he'd treated her mother.

Rick must have noticed something in her behavior because he quickly ended that conversation and moved on to introduce her to others he knew. He kept her hand in his, squeezing it gently when she tried to remove it.

When one of the businessmen asked her her profession, she reluctantly said she was studying for her doctorate. Of course, the next question was her field of study. She said, "Psychology."

"Who is your supervisory professor?"

"Dr. Cavanaugh."

"Why, he's here tonight. He'll be glad to know you know the star of the evening. Rick Austin is important in the business world."

"Yes, I believe he is." Vanessa forced herself not to look around for Dr. Cavanaugh. She felt sure he'd find her before she left. It seemed like destiny.

Rick put a hand on the small of her back. "I believe we should be seated so they can start serving."

He led her to their seats and Vanessa wanted to turn around and run out of the ballroom when she saw where they would be sitting. Up on stage where everyone—including Dr. Cavanaugh—could see them.

Yes, she would definitely be talking to her supervisor very soon.

She followed Rick to the dais, trying to think of how she could get out of taking a seat up there. Somehow she didn't think claiming a fear of heights would work. Nor could she manage to throw up before she reached her seat. And once she was there, there was no point to claiming illness. It would be too late.

Once they were seated, the master of ceremonies introduced the head table, including her, noting that she was Herbert Shaw's daughter. Apparently her father had been a longtime member of their group.

Vanessa tried to maintain a pleasant smile, glad when the spotlight moved down the table.

After it had done so, Rick leaned over. "Are you okay?"

"Yes, of course."

After they finished their delicious meal, Rick was

again introduced, and highlights of his impressive résumé were read aloud. Vanessa learned some new facts about Rick. She'd had no idea he'd earned his MBA from Harvard, or that he had studied in England. No wonder he had no time for a social life. He had accomplished more in ten years than most people did in a lifetime.

To her surprise, she enjoyed his speech very much. He included a sense of humor, sometimes self-deprecating, and fascinating stories about the people of China. When he finished, there was a roar of applause.

As he sat down, Vanessa whispered, "Well done."

He smiled and caught her hand, bringing it to his lips before she realized what he was doing. She jerked her hand away and ducked her head.

"What's wrong?"

"Nothing! Just—just don't do anything romantic here in front of everyone."

"Why?"

"Because my supervisory professor is here."

"You're not allowed romance if you're a psychology student?"

"Not if he's kin to a patient."

Rick frowned. Then it struck him. "Lindy," he said.

"Bingo."

They made it all the way through the salad course before her professor came forward asking Vanessa to introduce Rick. "I'm delighted to meet you, Mr.

Austin. I believe I spoke with your attorney about your sister."

"My *ex*-attorney," Rick corrected him, shaking his hand. "And I'm indebted to you for your quick solution."

"Your sister is doing well?"

"Yes, she is, thanks to Miss Shaw."

"I'm pleased to hear that. Oh, dear?" he called to a woman standing near him. "Come meet Mr. Austin and Vanessa Shaw. This is my wife, Joanna. I'm sure you've heard me mention Vanessa. She's one of my students in the doctorate program."

"Yes, of course. He raves about you, my dear. And, Mr. Austin, that was a most wonderful speech. I really enjoyed it."

"Thank you, Mrs. Cavanaugh."

"Oh, my dear," the older woman exclaimed to Vanessa, "that is such a beautiful bracelet. So unusual. Where did you find it?"

Vanessa glanced at the bracelet and wanted to hide it, but she couldn't. "A friend gave it to me."

"How lucky for you."

"Yes, it was."

Rick said, "If you'll excuse us, there are a couple more people I want to introduce Vanessa to. I'm delighted to meet both of you, though." He led Vanessa away.

"Thank you," she muttered when they were out of earshot.

"Yeah, I didn't think you wanted to tell them I brought you that bracelet."

"No. I think Dr. Cavanaugh might not believe it was for taking care of Lindy."

"It wasn't."

"Rick!" she exclaimed, a warning in her voice.

Rick surprised her by tugging her to the small dance floor. "Come on, let's dance."

"We shouldn't—" But she stopped because they were already on the dance floor with Rick's arms around her. "I thought you wouldn't do anything else romantic."

"Lots of people are dancing. It's an accepted social activity. Besides, it was either dance with you or kiss you. Did I make the right choice?"

"Yes!" She didn't confess that she was enjoying the dancing, but she was. It was the first time they'd danced together.

"Vanessa, when those people mentioned your father, you didn't appear happy. Was he mean to you?"

"No, just controlling. And Mom and I both placed low on his importance list. His work was everything to him."

Rick frowned. "He had his priorities screwed up."

Vanessa relaxed just a little more. "Your father wasn't like that?"

"Nope. When Mom was alive, she always came first. And he had time for me, too. After Mom died, I think he was lost. I was furious when he married

Anita, but I think he thought that marriage would be like his first one. Unfortunately he didn't get so lucky the second time."

"So, when you marry your wife will come first?" Vanessa asked, as if she had no idea who that person might be.

"Oh, yeah, honey, you'll come first," he said, and spun her around in a dizzying move.

"I didn't mean—" she began breathlessly.

"I did. And if I don't get to claim you soon, I may go crazy."

"Rick, you know we can't—"

"I know," he agreed with a sigh. "But it's hard."

"Yes, it is," she said softly, for her ears only. But he heard her. She could tell by the way he pressed her more tightly against him.

When the music ended, he suggested another dance, but Vanessa didn't think she could stand so much closeness without embarrassing herself. He led her off the floor.

They immediately ran into someone else Rick knew. "Mr. Nelson, how nice to see you," Rick said as a white-haired man approached him. "Allow me to introduce Miss Vanessa Shaw."

"Knew her daddy. Liked her mother better," the old man said.

Vanessa smiled. "Me, too."

"Smart young lady."

"Yes, she is," Rick agreed.

"Good. Like her better than that last one you brought to that meeting a couple of months ago."

"I do, too."

"Good. Better grab her while you can!"

"I couldn't agree more. I've just got to convince her." Rick gave her a smile.

Vanessa elbowed him in the ribs while keeping a smile on her lips.

The old man chuckled. "Feisty, isn't she? That kind makes the best wife."

"I agree, but I think you're embarrassing her."

"No reason to be embarrassed, missy. I'm complimenting you."

Still, Vanessa couldn't help the blush that colored her cheeks. "But I have all kinds of faults, Mr. Nelson. I'd just rather not admit them."

"Good thing to do. Keep quiet."

Then the old man leaned in closer to Rick and muttered, "Don't let this one get away."

"No, sir, I won't." Rick smiled.

As Rick led her away, Vanessa couldn't hold back any longer. "Rick, you need to be careful what you say. Someone might hear you!"

Rick just smiled down at her.

"Did you hear me?"

"I did. But I'm not saying anything I regret."

Vanessa just groaned. The man refused to listen to reason.

When the evening finally ended, they retrieved

their car and started home. "Your supervisory professor seemed very nice," Rick said.

"To you, perhaps. Monday, I'm sure he won't be as kind to me."

"Why?"

"Because he thinks I'm dating you and treating Lindy at the same time."

"And that's wrong?"

"It can be considered so. You can't date patients, or relatives if it would cause problems for the patient."

"But it's not causing any problems for Lindy," Rick said.

"No, because we're not dating."

Rick parked the car in front of Vanessa's home and turned to look at her. "You don't call this dating?"

"I wouldn't think it would be a good idea to date one woman while having a baby with another."

"Normally, I wouldn't, either. But I'm not going to marry Sharon, whether she's carrying my child or not, as I told you."

"That's easy to say now, when you don't know if it's your baby."

"It's easy for me to say because you pointed out how much alike Anita and Sharon are. I saw my father's life ruined because he married a woman he'd been sleeping with. I don't intend to make the same mistake."

"So you'd abandon your child to Sharon's care?"

"No. That's what I was explaining to Lindy this evening. I'd pay her enough money to get her to surrender custody to me. My only problem would be persuading the woman I want to marry to raise Sharon's child. Do you think that would be possible?"

"I wouldn't know," Vanessa said coolly.

"Come on, Vanessa. You know I'm talking about you. I've made it as clear as I can without actually asking you to marry me. I figured you'd prefer that I wait until I find out about the baby. I'm not sure I can wait that long, though, so I'm hoping Will and Jim will be able to clear things up long before the baby is born."

"I don't think you're aware of the significance of Dr. Cavanaugh being there this evening. He's going to ask me if I'm serious about you. I'm going to have to say I was just doing you a favor. That I have no emotional attachment to you. Otherwise, he may decide to deny me my doctorate."

"Why would he do that?"

"I told you. It might compromise the effectiveness of my work with Lindy."

"But it wouldn't. Lindy loves both of us. Why wouldn't she want us to get together and share our lives with her?"

"What if she fears I may not care for her as much as I did, because I'm in love with you."

"Are you?"

"Am I what?"

"In love with me?"

Vanessa felt her cheeks burn and she looked away.

She wouldn't answer his question. She couldn't. Instead she took a different approach. "Rick, I've worked for four years on my advanced degree. I have six more months of work. Then I'll be able to pursue the career I love."

"Okay," he said with a sigh. "Six months isn't forever."

"Thank you."

They sat in silence for several minutes. Finally, Rick said, "I'll agree to wait until your degree is safe, if you'll agree to kiss me good-night tonight."

"One kiss?"

"Sure."

Vanessa thought there must be some trap in the agreement, but after all, she had agreed. She slid closer to him and wrapped her arms around his neck. Then she lifted her lips to his.

As he pulled her tighter against him, his strength and his warmth overwhelmed her, and his lips demanded more. She found herself responding with enthusiasm. His hands started stroking her body, awakening feelings she hadn't experienced before.

When his lips left hers to trace kisses down her neck, she took a deep breath and started to protest, but his lips returned to hers, distracting her once again. Just as she was drowning in Rick's arms, she made one last desperate effort to break free, pushing him away.

Rick raised his head, but he kept his arms around her. "What?"

"We—we have to stop!" she gasped.

"Why?" he asked as his lips lowered to hers.

She ducked her head. "Because I'm too close to losing control."

"Me, too," he agreed, but he still tried to reach her lips.

"Rick, stop!"

He bowed his forehead against hers. "Okay, but I suggest you double your study efforts to finish early. Six months seems too long."

"I know," she whispered. They were the most encouraging words he'd yet heard.

He moved her away from him and opened his door, then came around the car and opened her door. He reached in and pulled her out of the car. Then he embraced her once more, exacting one more kiss before he led her to the house.

"Are you going to invite me in for coffee?" he asked.

"No, I don't think so. I think we've risked too much already tonight."

"Yeah, but it was sweet."

She didn't answer. Reaching for the door, she said, "Goodbye, Rick."

"Oh, no you don't. I get my goodbye kiss."

"I thought we—" His lips stopped her words.

He finally released her again. "Good night, Vanessa."

And he turned and walked away.

Vanessa stood there watching him go. Only after

he'd driven away did she open the door to her home. Betty had left an inside light on for her. She locked the door behind her and wandered slowly down the hall.

"Vanessa, is that you?"

Vanessa turned in to the library to greet Will. "Yes, it's me, Will. Why are you still up?"

"Your mother was a little nervous about going to bed before you got home. I promised to stay up for you so she'd get some sleep."

Vanessa was surprised. "I didn't think she had waited up for me in years."

"You haven't dated much the past couple of years."

She nodded. That was true. "I've been too busy, I guess."

Will led her into the kitchen for a cup of coffee he said Betty had brewed right before she went to bed. "How'd the evening go?" he asked after he'd poured them each a cup.

She sipped her decaf as she told Will about Dr. Cavanaugh and her concerns. Skipping the details of the sensuous dances and the heated kisses, of course.

"You explained the problem to Rick?" Will asked.

She nodded. "He was reluctant but he finally agreed. Not enthusiastically, I might add." Putting down the cup, she let out a deep sigh. "For some reason he seems to think we're dating. We aren't. I only agreed to fill in tonight because he didn't have anyone else." She put on her best face, sure she'd convinced Will.

If only she could convince herself…

But Will didn't fall for her story, either. As if in slow motion, a big grin split his face. "Yeah, right."

"Will!"

"Honey, I'll pretend to believe there's nothing between you and Rick Austin, if that's what you want. But we both know that's not true."

She looked at the man who'd been more a father to her than her own, and knew she could never fool him. Nor could she go on fooling herself.

"Am I that obvious?"

Chapter Fourteen

Vanessa had a restless night. But when she got up the next morning, she had made some decisions.

As she French-braided Lindy's blond hair, she put her first plan into action. "Lindy, I think it's time," she said gently. "I think you should start seeing a private therapist."

The teen's face expressed anxiety. "You don't want to be my therapist anymore?"

Vanessa reassured her with a brief hug. "Technically, sweetheart, I never was your therapist. I've given you a place to call home, taken care of you, loved you—" she smiled at the girl "—but you need a therapist to work through what your mother did to you."

She continued to braid Lindy's hair, doing it exactly the way she knew the girl liked it. "And," she added, "since Rick is now part of your family and I know him, too…well, things are…getting complicated."

"I understand," Lindy said. "I think."

"There's a lady who was my mentor a couple of years ago. She's got an office near here. I could set you up with a session once a week with her."

"And then I could come home and talk to you about it?"

"You can always talk to me." Vanessa smiled at Lindy in the mirror. "You know, her office is right across from a manicure shop. What do you say we both treat ourselves?"

Lindy agreed enthusiastically. She got even more excited when Vanessa suggested she have some of her friends over for a slumber party next Friday night.

"Could we stay up till eleven?" Lindy asked.

Vanessa laughed. "Good heavens, no. You don't sleep at all at a slumber party. Just wait and see."

They made plans and Vanessa felt positive. She'd done a good thing for Lindy.

But had she done the same for herself by clearing the obstacle to a relationship with Rick? There was still the problem with Sharon's baby to contend with, but the path was clearer now.

Would she take it?

RICK THOUGHT A LOT about what Vanessa had told him Saturday night. He was pretty sure that waiting six months for her doctorate would drive him crazy. Ten minutes with her in his arms had him wanting much more. And spending yesterday with her at her family dinner had been an exercise in self-control.

All through the meal he could only think about taking her into an empty room and kissing her.

He had a problem.

As he did with every difficulty that presented itself, on Monday Rick set out to overcome that problem. He knew Vanessa was doing her best for Lindy. So he needed to attack the other end of the problem. Dr. Cavanaugh. He figured out how much he could donate to charity for the year, wrote a check to the university and put it in an envelope with a letter addressed to Dr. Cavanaugh, explaining how pleased they were with Vanessa Shaw's handling of the situation. The letter expressed the hope that he would continue to see Ms. Shaw as a member of the university Psychology Department.

Not terribly subtle, but he wasn't in the mood for subtlety.

With that problem dealt with, he set out to take care of his own problem. He dialed Jeff Jacobs's office.

"Jeff, it's Rick Austin. Have we made any progress?"

"Well, Jim has found the guy Sharon dated, but he's out of town until today."

"Did Sharon go with him?"

"No. She's still trying to cause trouble. When I told her your terms, she stormed out of here, vowing you would pay."

"When was that?"

"Friday."

"Okay. I've got to protect Vanessa and Lindy from her. I don't want them to suffer because of me."

"I think those two can manage Sharon just fine. But if you want me to call Sharon and warn her off, I'll be glad to do so."

"No, you're right. I'm just anxious to get everything settled."

"We should make some real strides today or tomorrow. I'll call you as soon as I know something."

"I'll be waiting."

WHEN VANESSA REACHED her office on Monday morning after dropping an overly excited Lindy at her school, she found herself hoping Lindy wouldn't interrupt class with her social plans. However, a note on Vanessa's desk asking her to go to Dr. Cavanaugh's office as soon as she arrived helped her focus on her own situation. After putting down her briefcase, she walked down the hall and knocked on Dr. Cavanaugh's door.

"Come in."

"Good morning, Dr. Cavanaugh."

"Morning, Vanessa. I was delighted to see you Saturday evening."

"Yes, sir, and I was pleased to meet your wife."

He smiled and nodded. "I was, however, concerned to see you were escorted by Rick Austin. Are you still working with his sister?"

Here it comes, Vanessa thought. Good thing she'd

prepared for it. "Yes, sir, but not necessarily as a therapist. I'm more a family-figure. She lives with me and my parents and little brother."

Dr. Cavanaugh sat back and steepled his fingers in front of him. He looked pensive. "Don't you think she should be in therapy, since she attempted to take her life?"

"Yes, sir, and now I think she's ready. You see, her mother was incredibly neglectful. Anita spent all the money she was receiving on herself. Now that I've shown Lindy how a real family lives, I think she needs to begin therapy. I want her to go to Shelby Walters."

The doctor gave one nod, barely perceptible. But Vanessa was alert for any sign to give away his thoughts. "Excellent choice. She will continue to live with you?"

"Yes, and that's the reason for her seeing Shelby. Because she's more like a part of my family, she needs to talk to someone else."

"And she's okay with that?"

"Yes."

"I was concerned that you might've gotten too involved with the family while trying to provide therapy. That wouldn't have been professional."

"I agree."

"Well, I'm glad we had this little talk. I feel much better about everything."

"Me, too. Thank you, Dr. Cavanaugh."

She scooted out of his office before he could ask

anything else. Then she picked up the phone and called Shelby Walters. When the woman answered, they chatted for a couple of minutes. Then Vanessa got down to the point of the call.

"I have a patient I'd like to send to you for therapy." She gave all the details of Lindy's life. She discovered Shelby had a Monday afternoon appointment available and she signed Lindy up at once.

"All right, Vanessa. I'm delighted. Are you still on track to finish in six months?"

"Yes, I am. Especially with you helping Lindy. She'll still be living with me, but I didn't think I should be her therapist, as well."

"That's wise. I'll see you and Lindy next Monday."

Vanessa hung up the phone and breathed a sigh of relief. She thought she had avoided the difficulty with Dr. Cavanaugh, but she wasn't sure she would tell Rick yet. She wanted him to figure out what was happening with Sharon before they began to look to the future.

After teaching two classes and completing some paperwork, she packed up and headed back to the house. She stopped off at the nearest movie rental place and picked out three movies for the slumber party.

When she got home, Betty came out to meet her, saying lunch would be ready in a few minutes and, oh, by the way, Lindy had called to say the party was a go for Friday night. She'd spoken to all her friends.

"Big surprise!" Vanessa said. "I wasn't worried

about that." She looked around the kitchen. "Is Mom down for lunch?"

"Yes, but she's not feeling so good. I tried to get her to go to the doctor, but she's waiting for you."

Vanessa hurried to the morning room. "Mom?" she called as she entered. She found her mother lying on the sofa. "Are you all right?"

"I'm not feeling very well," her mother admitted.

"Where do you hurt?"

"My head, my stomach. I don't know if it's indigestion or something else."

"I'm calling the doctor."

Though Vivian balked her protests were weak. In no time Vanessa contacted the doctor, who told her to bring Vivian in at once. Vanessa made one other call—to Will.

When they reached the doctor's office, Will was already there waiting. Vanessa let her mother sit down with him while she signed her in.

"Do you mind if I stay?" she asked Will.

"Of course not. Your mom would want that."

"Thanks, Will."

"When did she start feeling bad?"

"I don't know. When I came home from school, Betty told me she wasn't feeling well but had insisted on waiting until I got home to call the doctor."

"I'm not dead yet," Vivian said. "I can hear you talking about me."

Will obliged her. "Okay, so why did you wait for

Vanessa? Peter could've driven you. I could've come to get you."

Vivian shrugged. "I just didn't feel quite right. It's not like I have a specific pain."

"Okay, sweetheart. I won't fuss at you anymore." He wrapped his arms around her and comforted her.

When the doctor was ready for them, Vanessa stayed in the waiting room. They weren't long. When they came out, she could see her mother had been crying. Her chest tightened and she ran across the room. "What's wrong?"

"He's not sure," Will replied, "but he wants her to stay in bed for a week and then come back and see him."

"Okay. We can do that. Betty won't mind climbing the stairs."

"I can carry her down before I go to work each morning so she'll be in the morning room. Then when I get home, I'll carry her back up."

"Yes, if she feels up to it. I think she should be taking naps every day. And she can do that better in your room."

"We'll see what she feels like doing. If you'll take her home and settle her on the couch, I'm going to run by the office and gather up some papers so I can come home and work while she rests."

"Of course. Come on, Mom, let's go. I'm sure Betty is worried about you."

By the time they got home, Betty had lined the sofa with a comforter and several pillows. When

Vivian saw her housekeeper's thoughtfulness, she almost burst into tears.

"Oh, Betty, you are so sweet."

"Now, now, Miss Vivian, don't you be crying. Mr. Will would get after me if he thought I made you cry."

Vivian laughed, as she was meant to do, as Vanessa eased her back against the pillows.

"Why don't you eat some of the lunch Betty made? It's your favorite—meat loaf."

Vivian thanked her again for her thoughtfulness, then Betty left them alone.

As her mother ate, they chatted about trivial things. It only took a few minutes for Vivian to eat her fill.

"You don't want any more, Mom?"

"No, honey. I think I'll just take a nap."

Vanessa picked up the dishes and headed to the kitchen. There she sat and ate her lunch, telling Betty and Peter about the doctor's orders.

"I think we just need to keep everything quiet for her," Betty said.

"That'll be hard if you have a slumber party," Peter reminded them.

"Oh, no!" Vanessa said with a gasp. "Lindy was so excited today. What are we going to do?"

"I'm afraid we'll have to disappoint her. We can't let her have a slumber party while Miss Vivian isn't feeling good."

"I know. I suppose I could rent a hotel room, but that wouldn't be like a real slumber party."

"Why don't you let her go to Mr. Rick's house?" Peter suggested. "Mrs. Abby would take care of them."

"And I could send some treats with them," Betty added, smiling.

Slowly, Vanessa said, "I guess we could do that. I could go keep an eye on them. Rick might even be out of town. That would be best. Let me go call Mrs. Abby."

When she got Rick's housekeeper on the phone, she explained the situation to her. Mrs. Abby was delighted to host the slumber party at her house.

"Will Rick be in town?" Vanessa asked.

"Oh, yes, he's been in town since he got back from China."

"Then I guess I'd better call him and make sure he won't mind."

"I'm sure he won't, Vanessa, but it'd be best to check with him."

"All right, Mrs. Abby. Thank you for agreeing."

She hung up the phone and drew a deep breath. Then she called Rick's office. When she asked to talk to him, the secretary asked who was calling. She gave her name, wondering if Rick would take her call. Almost at once, he came on the line.

"Hi, Vanessa. What a nice surprise."

Vanessa got right down to business. "I need to ask you if Lindy could hold her slumber party at your house Friday night. Mom isn't feeling well and the doctor wants her to get lots of rest. We're afraid Lindy's party might cause too much noise."

"I'd be in charge of a bunch of teenage girls?" Rick sounded terrified.

"No, sorry, I forgot to say I'd come stay at your house to keep an eye on them."

"Good, and I can keep an eye on you. I've been trying to come up with a reason to see you again, and you've just handed me one."

"It's for Mom, Rick, not for you."

"I think it works for me as well as your mom. I'll call Mrs. Abby—"

"I already asked her. We didn't want to approach you if she had a problem with it."

"Then we're on for Friday night."

"The girls will want to order pizza for dinner. I forgot to tell Mrs. Abby that. But she can fix some snacks for them and I'm sure Betty will send some over with me. I've rented three movies, but it will take them a while to settle down, I'm sure."

"I don't care what they do. I'll be entertaining you."

"*We* will be keeping an eye on the girls."

"You're trying to ruin all my fun, aren't you."

"Someone's got to keep you in line."

"Uh-huh. Okay, give Vivian my best. I'll talk to you later."

"Rick, I really do appreciate this."

"I'm happy to do it for Lindy. And for me."

Chapter Fifteen

Vanessa didn't know which of them was looking forward to Friday more—her or Lindy.

When the day finally came, Vanessa thought she'd never get Lindy into school. On the ride there, the girl talked incessantly about the slumber party.

On the way to the university, Vanessa was alone with her thoughts, and they bombarded her from all angles. They all had one thing in common. Rick.

Tonight she and Rick would chaperone the party. She wasn't sure that would work, especially since they would be alone together for a good part of the night. After all, they wouldn't want to impose their presence on the girls unless there was a problem. Then she remembered Mrs. Abby. Of course the housekeeper would be around. Vanessa could make sure she stayed with Mrs. Abby so that Rick couldn't lure her into a complicated situation. She was afraid she couldn't resist temptation if he did.

She struggled with her classes that day, finding it difficult to keep her mind on her teaching. Somehow, everything they studied seemed to link itself to Rick.

When she finally got back to her office, she decided that since it was Friday, she would just go on home. She wanted to check on her mother and get ready for the evening.

Just as she was packing up to go, Dr. Cavanaugh knocked on her door. The door was open, so she couldn't pretend she wasn't there.

"Yes, Dr. Cavanaugh?"

"I have something I want to show you."

He handed an envelope to her. When she saw the letter was from the Austin Group, she was fearful of what she would find. Surely Rick hadn't complained about their relationship. But she worried that he might have confessed to a greater involvement than she had admitted to.

Her fingers were shaking as she pulled out a single sheet of paper. She opened the folded letter and something fell out on her desk: a check for one million dollars. With a gasp, she stared at Dr. Cavanaugh. "What—what is this?"

"A check obviously. Read the letter."

She did, and when she finished, she breathed a sigh of relief. Rick had certainly praised her behavior, but he hadn't revealed anything between them.

"Vanessa, I wondered if you knew why he wrote the letter and included the check."

"I—I might have warned him about any personal relationship with Lindy or her family as long as I was treating her."

"Very proper. And is the possibility of that happening the reason you asked Shelby to take on Lindy as a patient?"

She couldn't lie. Not only couldn't she live with herself if she did, but Dr. Cavanaugh would see right through her. "Yes, it is," she said faintly.

She braced herself for his admonishment.

Instead, Dr. Cavanaugh said, "That was a thoughtful solution. I could tell there was something between you and Rick."

She could hardly believe her ears. Struggling to maintain a professional demeanor and not jump for joy, she looked up at him. "I'm glad you think so, sir. So should I tear up the check?"

Dr. Cavanaugh leaned over and snatched it up. "Not on your life! I have great plans for this money."

"But, Dr. Cavanaugh, he—"

"He wanted to thank us for offering immediate help. And you did a great job."

"Oh. But are you sure you should keep it?"

"Of course I am. Besides, as a romantic gesture I think it's highly impressive. I don't think he'd want us to tear it up."

"No, I guess not."

"Just tell him I appreciate his generosity when you see him next."

"Yes. I'll see him tonight."

"Now, I'm off to the bank!"

After her supervisor left her office, Vanessa slumped over her desk and rested her head on her arms. A romantic gesture? Yes, it was huge. She'd waited patiently all week for him to call her and give her an update on his problem. But it was Friday and she hadn't heard anything. She didn't want to ask Will again.

Of course, she hadn't bothered to tell Rick she'd sorted out her problem without his generous donation. So when she finally told him her degree was not in jeopardy, he might be angry with her.

Why was their romance so complicated?

That was a foolish question. With Lindy and Sharon in the mix, it had to be complicated. And she knew her reluctance to be involved, in spite of the attraction she felt, had made things difficult, too.

That was an understatement!

She raised her head and packed the last of her papers in her briefcase. Time to go home, check on her mother and Danny, and maybe get some rest before she set out for the sleepover.

AT HOME, Vivian was lying down on the sofa in the morning room. When her mother looked up, she asked, "How are you feeling?"

"Bored. I've rested long enough."

"I know, but you don't see the doctor till Monday. You have to wait until then."

"I'm so sorry you had to move the slumber party to Rick's house. I feel like I let everyone down."

"You're being silly, Mom. We all know you didn't want to ruin Lindy's plans, but we also know that the baby is a lot more important than a slumber party."

"I know," Vivian said with a sigh. "By the way, have you heard anything about Rick's situation?"

"No, have you?"

"No. I asked Will once and he just kissed me and said nothing."

Vanessa sighed. She needed someone to talk to, and as always, her mother was here for her. "You remember I told you about Dr. Cavanaugh being at The Mansion that night?" At Vivian's nod, she continued. "I sorted it out with him by arranging for Lindy to see another therapist. But I didn't tell Rick that."

Her mother just listened, not passing judgment.

"I guess he was worried about it, because today Dr. Cavanaugh showed me a big check to the Psychology Department that Rick sent, along with a letter praising my work and saying he hoped I'd be associated with the department for many years."

"Oh, how wonderful of him."

"Yes. And now I feel a little guilty that I hadn't told him what I did."

"Maybe you shouldn't tell him?"

"I don't want to lie about anything to him. He— he's indicated he's serious about our future." She waited, breathless, for her mother's reaction.

"How do you feel about it?"

"I think I feel the same way."

Vivian reached up to hug her daughter. "I think he's a good man. And he certainly fits in well with our family."

"Mmm-hmm. And he's done a wonderful job with Lindy."

"With your help. The two of you didn't get off to such a great start."

"But even then there was something between us. I was resisting as hard as I could, but I didn't hold out long. I can't." She let herself smile.

Her mother took Vanessa's hands in hers. "I've worried about who you would marry. We've been so lucky with marriages in our family. It took me a second time to find the right guy, but I did. You were the last one, and I've been concerned about your future for a while now."

"Oh, Mom, you'd better worry about the little one you're bringing into the world. You've got Danny and the baby to marry off in a few years."

"I know. Time really flies. It seems like just last week that it was just the two of us. Now we are such a big family."

Vanessa laughed. "Not everyone, but we are getting bigger all the time."

"Oh, I forgot to tell you. Rachel called. She's pregnant again."

"Really?"

"Yes. It appears we conceived at almost the same time."

Vanessa laughed and backed up. "Maybe I'd better stay away from both of you in case it's catching."

"It's not us you need to stay away from to avoid pregnancy. It's Rick. I've seen the way he looks at you."

She chuckled, feeling lighthearted. "You could be right, Mom."

Just then Betty brought in lunch for the two of them. "I expect you both to clean your plates," she said before she left them.

Vivian stared at the loaded tray. "How does she expect me not to be overweight when I go to the doctor if I eat everything? Look at that coconut pie. She knows it's my favorite."

"Mine, too. We'll just do the best we can and then you can plead your appetite is off. And I'll say... What can I say?"

"You can say you're in love. Betty already knows that, and she approves too!"

"In that case, maybe we can go straight to the pie."

They had almost finished their lunches when the doorbell rang. Vanessa glanced at her mother. "Are you expecting anyone?"

"No. Not anyone who would come to the front door. Maybe it's Rick."

"I'll go see."

When she opened the door onto the hallway, she could hear Sharon's strident voice as Peter tried to close the front door on the woman. Vanessa went to assist him.

"Let me in!" Sharon screamed.

"What do you want?" Vanessa asked.

"I want revenge!"

"That's not going to make me let you in, Sharon. Besides, I haven't done anything."

"Oh yeah? You were the one who told him about Larry, weren't you?"

"So?"

"Larry's furious with me! He refuses to have anything to do with me now."

"He didn't know about Rick?"

"No! I didn't want— He's my—"

Sharon stopped talking because tears were falling from her eyes. For the first time, Vanessa felt sorry for her.

"Sharon, I'm not the reason Larry is mad at you. The fact that you tried to trick Rick with Larry's baby is your fault."

"Who told you that?"

"No one. I figured it out."

"Well, I'm going to kill you before you tell anyone else! You're not going to destroy all my plans!"

Peter, who had moved behind the door, out of sight, yelled, "Betty, call the police!"

But his order was too late.

Sharon pulled a gun and pointed it at Vanessa.

Vanessa jumped behind the door and gave it a

mighty shove. It knocked Sharon's hand and the gun went off, chipping the door. When the crazed woman bent down to recover the weapon, Vanessa pushed her over. Then she closed the door and locked it.

It all happened so quickly, Vanessa couldn't believe it. Her mother was coming down the hall, almost running, and Danny and Betty had emerged from the kitchen. Then a bullet struck a window in the front of the house, shattering the glass.

Gathering her wits, Vanessa guided everyone to the library. Its windows were narrow and looked out on the side of the house. She thought they would be safer there.

"Betty, did you call the police?" she shouted.

"I didn't have a chance."

Vanessa grabbed a phone and dialed 911. When the police answered, a bullet shattered another window.

"Ma'am, is that gunfire?" the police dispatcher asked.

"Yes, there's someone outside shooting the windows out. She tried to shoot me."

"We've got two cars on their way right now. Stay away from the windows."

Next Vivian called Will. She told him what was happening.

"I'm on my way. Stay away from the windows."

As if to underscore his words, another shot hit the house. They all cringed.

"I wish there was something I could do," Peter

said. "We should be able to stop her. I could slip out the back and attack her from the back and—."

"No!" Vivian shouted. "Will said to stay inside."

They realized that Sharon had figured out where they were, when she shot out one of the narrow library windows. Vanessa was the closest to it. The bullet didn't strike her, but shards of glass did. Her arm started bleeding.

Betty got up. "I'll go get some gauze and—"

Vanessa stopped her. "No, give me your apron, Betty. Now everybody get down on the floor behind a piece of furniture."

Peter crawled across the room with Betty's apron and wrapped it tightly around the cut.

"Thank you, Peter," Vanessa said softly.

Then they heard the sounds they were waiting for. Police sirens. Vanessa knew the barrage wouldn't last much longer. But, to her surprise, she heard more gunshots.

"Surely she isn't stupid enough to shoot at the police?" Vanessa asked no one in particular.

Then the shooting stopped as abruptly as it had started. After several moments of silence Vanessa knew the siege was over.

The doorbell rang, and Peter got up. "I'll answer it."

"Peter, make sure it's the police first," Vanessa said. "Do you want me to go with you?"

"No, Vanessa, you stay in here. Take care of the rest of them."

Just then they heard the screech of tires as a car pulled into the drive.

"That will be Will," Vivian said with confidence.

"Stay here until he comes in, Mom. We have to be sure."

Moments later the door swung open and Will searched the room with his gaze, looking for Vivian and Danny. He came to them at once. "Are you all right, sweetheart? Danny?"

Danny crawled into his daddy's arms. "It was scary, Daddy."

"I know, son, but Mommy and Vanessa took care of you, didn't they?"

"Yeah."

He looked over at Vanessa. "You're bleeding! Were you shot?"

"No, Will, it was glass from the window."

Jim appeared then in the doorway. "Everyone all right in here?"

"Vanessa has a wound from flying glass. We need to get it taken care of."

Her brother came to her. "Come on, Vanessa. There's an ambulance here. They can take care of you."

"I didn't know you'd come, Jim," Vanessa said, feeling a little better.

"With someone shooting at all of you, of course I came. Let me help you," he said, taking her wounded arm in his hands.

She was afraid to ask, but she had to know. "What happened to Sharon?"

"She started shooting at the policemen. They didn't have much choice."

"You mean...she's dead?" Vanessa asked, her voice rising.

"Maybe they just wounded her," Jim said.

"Oh, no, the baby!"

"You think that was Rick's baby?"

"It doesn't matter now," Vanessa said, tears starting down her cheeks.

When Jim led her out the front door, Peter was talking to one of the policemen. "Here's Vanessa. That woman tried to shoot her."

"What we don't know is why," the policeman stated.

Jim whispered to Vanessa, "Let me handle this." In a louder voice, he asked, "Can the EMTs bandage her arm? And while they do that, I think I can explain all this."

"We'd be interested in hearing that," the officer said as he waved for the EMTs to come to the front door.

"Can they take her into the kitchen? I think that would be the best place to work."

The EMTs immediately did as Jim asked and led Vanessa into the kitchen. After they sat her down at the table and unwrapped her arm, she asked, "The, uh, the shooter. Is she dead?"

"I'm afraid so." The man kept working on her arm.

Vanessa ducked her head, trying to conceal her tears.

"Wasn't she trying to kill you?"

Vanessa nodded but said nothing else. They finished the bandaging and she thanked them with as much sincerity as she could manage under the circumstances. She was shaken over Sharon's fate.

"Ma'am," the officer said, stepping into the kitchen, "did the lady say why she wanted to kill you?"

"There was a man she intended to marry, only he hadn't asked her. She thought he was going to ask me."

"And the man's name?"

"I don't think I want to tell you that."

"Is it the man in the hall?"

She shook her head.

"Ma'am, I think you need to tell us his name."

"Why? He hasn't done anything wrong."

"Are you sure about that?"

"Yes. Jim?" she called. She was relieved when her brother came into the kitchen. "This policeman keeps asking who was involved, but I don't think I should tell him."

"Me, neither. I'm not required to reveal a client."

She turned to the policeman. "I decline to tell you anything else."

"Not even the name of the shooter?"

"No, I can tell you that. Her name is Sharon Cresswell."

"Did she live in the area?"

With a sigh, Jim gave the policeman her home

address. Then he turned to Vanessa. "Have they finished with you?"

"I think so."

After the EMTs left the room Will stepped into the kitchen. "Did they take care of you, Vanessa?"

"Yes, Will, thank you. Is everyone all right?"

"I think so. I had Vivian call her doctor."

"Was she injured, sir?" the policeman asked.

"No, but she's pregnant. We want to make sure she is all right."

"I see. And do you know the gentleman who was involved in this shootout?"

"Of course I do, but he's our client, and we're not going to reveal his identity. He has done nothing wrong. He offered to pay the woman's medical bills and when the baby was born, he wanted a DNA test to ensure that he was the father."

"So she was pregnant?"

"We're not sure. The woman could have lied. We were investigating the situation."

"I see." The officer nodded. "You're sure that's all you can give us?"

"Yes, absolutely—" Will began, then they all heard noises outside the house.

Rick burst into the kitchen and snatched Vanessa up into his arms.

"Are you all right? Did she hurt you? Damn it, why didn't you call me?"

The policeman stepped forward. "So this would be the gentleman involved. May I ask your name, sir?"

"Certainly. I'm Rick Austin."

Chapter Sixteen

Vanessa loved the feel of Rick's arms around her. She lay back against him, wishing they were anywhere but here. That this entire tragedy hadn't happened.

But it had, and now Rick had gotten himself involved.

"We were trying to keep you out of it," she told him.

He looked down at her. "Why?"

"You're a client, and Will would've kept you confidential. Your business, your reputation…"

He silenced her with a hush. "My business and my reputation mean a lot to me," he said, "but not as much as you. And Lindy. And telling the truth about what happened. Besides, I didn't do anything wrong, except be a bit dense."

If Vanessa hadn't already realized she loved this man, she did then.

Rick looked up at the policeman, not letting her go. "The woman—Sharon—was claiming to be carrying my child. But we all doubt that." He shook his head, as if in disbelief. "I can't believe she tried to kill Vanessa. Have you taken her to jail?"

A silence fell over the room which Vanessa finally broke. In a low voice she said, "She's dead."

Rick looked at her but didn't speak.

"She fired on the policemen. They fired back."

Rick pulled her tightly against him again. "I feel sorry for her," he whispered. Then, "But she should never have pulled a stunt like this. I didn't realize she'd go this far." His brow creased and he asked, "But why did she come after you?"

"She thought if she killed me, I couldn't repeat that I thought she was using Larry's baby to scam you."

"Did she admit that?"

"No, but I took a chance and guessed."

"You took a big chance, sweetheart."

"I didn't have any idea that she would try to kill me. I guess I never realized, either, how desperate she was."

With a big sigh, Rick said, "Neither did I. Thank God you're all right." He buried himself in her embrace.

"Sir, we'd like to ask you a few questions," the policeman said, interrupting their quiet discussion.

Rick looked up and gathered himself. "I understand. But first I need to make sure she's resting. I'll be right back." He led Vanessa out of the kitchen and into the morning room.

"I'm fine, Rick," she protested. "I could've stayed in there and helped you."

"I'll be fine. Besides, Will and Jim will be there. You need to rest and it wouldn't hurt if you took something for the pain."

"I might fall asleep," she said, as if that would be horrible.

"That wouldn't be a bad thing. We still have the slumber party tonight."

"Oh I'd forgotten that. We can't—" But how could she disappoint Lindy? Besides, the party might be a pleasant diversion from the horrors of today. "I guess we have to go through with it."

"Not if you don't want to."

"No, I couldn't do that to Lindy."

He kissed her. "We'll see. We've got a few hours before we have to make a final decision."

By that time they had reached the morning room. They found Vivian lying down on the sofa and Betty entertaining Danny. The little boy immediately looked up to see who was coming in. They both saw the disappointment on his face. But he came running to them.

"Have you seen my daddy? Is he okay?"

Rick knelt to the little boy's level. "Your daddy is safe, Danny, I promise. He's just talking to the police so your mommy won't have to."

"Can I go help him?"

"I think you'd better wait here until he comes back."

"Okay." It was clear Danny wanted to say something else, so Rick waited.

"Were you scared?" the boy finally asked.

"Yes, I was." Rick took Danny's hands in his own. "You know, it's perfectly normal to be scared in a dangerous situation."

"Oh, I was scared."

"So was I," Vanessa added, hunkering down to her brother's level.

"'Nessa, I'm glad you're okay. 'Cause you bleeded a lot."

"Yes, I did, but now I have a pretty bandage. See?"

"Do I get to sign it?"

"No, sweetheart. It's not hard, like a cast. It's just a bandage."

"Danny, you'd better come back over here and play with your trucks," Betty suggested.

When the boy did as he was told, Vanessa checked on her mother, for her own peace of mind. "Mom, are you okay?"

"Yes, honey, and the doctor said the baby should be, too. He told me to rest. But so far I feel great. Mostly I feel relieved that you weren't shot."

"Me, too," Rick said, putting his arm around Vanessa again. "It kind of puts things in perspective, doesn't it."

"It does," Vivian agreed.

"I promised the policeman I'd come back to the kitchen and answer questions, but I thought Vanessa needed to sit down and take some aspirin for the pain."

Betty jumped up. "I'll go get it."

"Thanks, Betty," Rick said as he settled Vanessa in a large, comfortable chair. He fussed over her.

"I'm not an invalid, Rick. I just cut my arm."

"I know. But I still think you should go to your doctor, just to be sure you don't need stitches."

"I'm fine," she repeated patiently. "Now you just be careful yourself when you talk to the police."

He smiled at her—that smile she loved. "If I managed not to offend anyone in China, I think I can handle an interview in my own language." Then he kissed her again and walked out of the room.

Betty returned. "Take your aspirin now, Vanessa."

To tell the truth, she was feeling her cuts more than she'd thought she would.

"Just lie back and relax," Betty ordered. "We've had a trying day."

"Yes, we have." Vanessa couldn't believe the events of the past few hours. It was as if she'd dreamed them. No, she corrected herself. They were more like a nightmare.

But the nightmare was over.

"I don't really need to rest," she told Betty, even as she did what the older woman had suggested.

That was the last thing she remembered for several hours.

VANESSA COULDN'T REMEMBER why she was sleeping in a big stuffed chair in the morning room when Will awakened her. Then it hit her. *Sharon.*

With a groan, she slumped back in the chair.

"Are you all right, Vanessa?" Will asked.

She struggled up again. "Yes, of course. It was just—just shocking."

"Yes, it was. But you did everything right. Peter told me all that happened. And he said you saved all their lives by getting the door closed on Sharon."

"I know. But…I didn't want her death."

"No one did. But Sharon brought that on herself."

Vanessa nodded. In her mind she knew Will was right, but her heart told a different version. "What time is it?" she asked him.

"It's almost three. The girls will be at Rick's by four o'clock. Are you going to go ahead and have the sleepover?"

"Yes, of course. I don't want to disappoint Lindy."

"Okay. Mrs. Abby called, and I said I'd have you call her."

"I'll do that at once."

When she called Rick's housekeeper, Mrs. Abby was greatly relieved to hear from her. "Rick told me you were all right, but it sounded like a terrible experience."

"It was. But I want Lindy to have her sleepover. Is it still all right with you?"

"Oh my, yes, I haven't suffered any stress. I'll be ready for you when you get here."

"All right. I'll be there before four."

After that, she went upstairs and took a shower. She braided her hair as she had Lindy's earlier. Then she donned jeans and a cotton sweater. She was beginning to feel more like herself—as long as she didn't think of Sharon.

After she was ready, she went to the kitchen to see what Betty had made for the sleepover. As usual, Betty had outdone herself. She had brownies and cookies, and even small uncooked quiches.

"Mrs. Abby can serve these for a snack or for breakfast in the morning."

"All right. I'll tell her. Thank you, Betty."

"I need to thank you for helping my Peter," Betty said past a tight throat, obviously trying not to cry.

"Peter and I worked together. I couldn't have done it without his help." She hugged Betty and then picked up all she had prepared. "I'll see you tomorrow morning."

After kissing Betty on the cheek, she headed to her car, trying not to look around and think about what had happened here that day. Instead, she pulled the car away, with high hopes for the night.

RICK WAS QUITE PLEASED with himself when he left the jewelry store at three. He'd looked at every ring they had. Finally, he'd found the one that looked right to him. It was in his pocket.

He started to go back to the office, then, realizing he needed to be home before the girls came at four, he headed there. Besides, he couldn't wait to see Vanessa.

Vanessa arrived right after him, pulling into the drive behind his Mercedes.

As she came around the car, he pulled her into his arms and kissed her, without saying a word.

She broke off the kiss before it deepened. "What if someone sees us?" she asked, looking around.

"Why would we care?"

"If my teenager was going to a sleepover, I would be concerned if the chaperones were too focused on each other."

"Oh, the sleepover. Is that why you're here? I thought it was for some other reason."

Vanessa smiled at the lascivious grin he shot her. "I need to get some things that Betty sent out of my car."

"I'll help you."

He carried in a tray as well as a bag of movies. "I don't even know these titles," he said, peeking inside.

Vanessa defended her selections. "They're good stories that the girls will love."

"I'm not sure they'll even watch them. Don't you have an action movie? Something with big explosions?"

"For teenage girls? Are you crazy?"

"Do *I* have to watch them?"

"What else are you going to do?"

He gave her that grin again. "Well, I had in mind a little one-on-one."

"Not when the girls will walk in on us at any minute."

When they reached the kitchen, Mrs. Abby welcomed them. "I'm glad you got here before the girls."

Vanessa agreed. "Once they get started, they're hard to settle down."

They set to work and at four o'clock exactly they had everything arranged, including a cooler with sodas, and two air mattresses in front of the big-screen TV in the den.

"I don't think we should mention anything about today's events," Rick said, suddenly getting serious. "It would upset Lindy."

"I'll think up another reason for my bandage."

Just then the doorbell rang, and Mrs. Abby answered it to eight young ladies, squealing and giggling in excitement as all teenagers do.

"Come right in," Mrs. Abby said as she waved them through. A couple of mothers were standing behind the girls. "We wanted to be sure Miss Shaw would be here," one of them said. "We heard about what happened today."

"Vanessa?" Mrs. Abby called to her as she welcomed the girls. "Can you come over here?"

Vanessa hurried over and met the two mothers. "Yes, I'm here. Everything is fine."

"We didn't say anything to the girls."

After Vanessa reassured the two mothers they left, and she rejoined the girls and Rick. Once the pizza arrived, she popped one of the movies into the DVD player and sat back.

Rick watched the movie, though he didn't admit to liking it. Vanessa couldn't help but smile at that.

When the girls moved on to the next one, he had other ideas. "I'd rather be alone with you," he told Vanessa. "Mrs. Abby can call if the girls need us."

"Call? Where are we going?"

"Just to my dad's study. I think we need to leave the girls some time alone, you know."

"I agree," she said, as he led her by the hand into the other room.

Rick closed the door behind them. "I used to know I was in trouble when my dad closed the door. I figured I'd been so bad he didn't even want my mother to know. Sometimes, I couldn't figure out what I'd done, but I knew he'd tell me."

"He sounds like a really good father."

"He was. The only time he messed up was when he married Anita. He tried to make up for that later, but he was limited as to what he could do after they had Lindy—and Anita must have known that."

Vanessa nodded. "That's the usual thing a gold-digger does. She has a child and then has a hold on the guy for the rest of his life."

"I want to have children, but not for that reason. Do you want children?"

"Yes, but not right away. I want to establish my career—"

Suddenly she looked stricken.

"What's wrong, honey? Are you afraid I'll push you to have children before you're ready?"

"No. I remembered something I was supposed to

tell you. Dr. Cavanaugh said for me to thank you for your generous donation. But I'd already taken care of the situation and I didn't tell you. I tried to get Dr. Cavanaugh to return the check, but he wouldn't."

"How did you fix it?"

"I set Lindy up with another therapist, a friend of mine."

He pulled her into his arms. "Good solution."

"You aren't mad at me?"

"No."

"Dr. Cavanaugh saw it as a romantic gesture. I thought it was, too."

"I don't care about the money. But I almost lost you today because I hadn't realized how dangerous Sharon had become."

"I knew she was on edge, too, and I'm the professional. Still, even if I had seen it, the police couldn't have arrested someone just because I thought they might be dangerous." She shook her head in frustration. "But I can't stop thinking I should have seen it coming."

Rick took her hands in his. "You can't blame yourself, Vanessa. And I for one think you'll make a great psychologist. Look what you've done for Lindy, and for me. You gave me back my sister, my family." He dropped a kiss on her lips. "You've changed me, made me see there's more to life than the Austin Group."

Tears glistened in her eyes when she looked up at him. "Thank you, Rick. That means a lot to me."

"There's nothing we can do about what's already happened, so I'm trying to put it behind me. Now I'm concentrating on the future." He reached into his pocket and felt for the ring box.

Just then someone knocked on the office door.

With a frown at the interruption, Rick opened the door to find Mrs. Abby standing there.

"Yes?"

"Someone named Jim is calling for you. He said it was important."

"Thanks, Mrs. Abby."

He picked up the desk phone. "Jim? It's Rick."

After several minutes, where Jim must have been doing all the talking, Rick hung up the phone.

"What did he say?" Vanessa asked, a worried expression on her face.

Rick gave her a brief kiss. "He said he has talked to Sharon's doctor, and she wasn't pregnant, as far as the doc knew. She apparently thought she could bluff her way through until after I paid her money."

Vanessa put her arms around Rick's neck and leaned against him. "I'm so relieved. I was so upset when—" She buried her face in Rick's chest as he held her close.

"I know, honey, I know." After a couple of minutes, he said, "Don't you want to see what I have here?" He showed her the ring box. "I know we said we were going to wait, but I don't *want* to wait any longer." He looked deep into her eyes. "Vanessa, will you marry me?"

She glanced at the box and then at his face. "Are you sure?"

"Very sure."

"Then, yes."

Rick gave her a brief hug and pulled back. "Don't you want to open the box? I want to show off my fiancée with a beautiful ring."

She took the box and flipped up the lid. "Oh, Rick, it's beautiful!"

"Not as beautiful as you," he said, and kissed her the way he'd been yearning to do all day. "Here, let's put it on your finger. I had to call your mom and get your ring size."

"It's a perfect fit."

Rick pulled her close and kissed his future bride. As enthralled as they were, a few minutes later it took several rings for them to realize they were hearing the phone again.

Rick muttered as he reached for the receiver, but said politely, "Hello?"

"May I speak to Vanessa, please?"

He handed the phone to her.

"Hello. Oh, Rachel! You saw it on television? Yes, I'm fine. No, everyone's fine. And Rick is especially fine," Vanessa said with a wink at Rick.

Rick stood there, his hands on his hips. That was what he got for proposing to a woman with as much family as Vanessa had. There would always be someone calling to be sure she was all right. But he'd make sure she was. As her husband, he would protect her—and any children they might have.

He was thrilled, though. He finally had a big family.

As he walked over to Vanessa, she motioned to her ring, clearly wondering if she could tell her sister. Rick grinned and nodded. He wanted the world to know.

When Vanessa got off the phone, she said, "Rachel was thrilled."

"I can't wait to meet her."

"Unfortunately they won't be coming to Dallas until after she's out of her first trimester."

Rick looked puzzled.

"Oh, I forgot to tell you she's pregnant, just like Mom."

"No, you hadn't told me that. But I hope you can get married without her, because I'm not interested in waiting long."

"Maybe she can make one short trip. How long did you have in mind?"

"How about next week?"

"Next week! But—"

He kissed her deeply.

When she surfaced, a smile lit her face. "Maybe we can make it next week."

Epilogue

It took a little longer than a week, but by the end of the month, a wedding took place in the morning room at the Greenfield house. It wasn't the first one, but to Rick and Vanessa it was very special.

Lindy, too, was excited. Not only would she get Vanessa as a permanent part of her family, but she would also get to move back into her own home after the honeymoon. Not that she wouldn't miss Vivian and Will, Danny and Betty and Peter, but they would be close. And she would be returning to where she began—part of the family again.

And today there was one other exciting thing. She was Vanessa's maid of honor. Her dress was a shimmering blue silk that looked great on her, if she did say so herself. Staring into the mirror, she couldn't believe how lucky she was.

"Are you ready?" Rebecca called through her door.

Lindy turned and grinned. "Yes, I don't think I could be more ready."

"Want to see the bride?"

"Is she ready?"

"Yes, and she looks beautiful."

When Rebecca opened Vanessa's door, Lindy gasped. "Oh, Vanessa, you look so beautiful! Rick is going to just melt right there at the altar."

Vanessa chuckled. "I hope not. There wouldn't be much of a honeymoon if that happened."

"It's time," Rebecca said. "Will's waiting for you at the bottom of the stairs."

"Okay. Go ahead, Lindy. I'll follow you."

As the girl left her bedroom, Vanessa turned and hugged her sister. "Rebecca, thank you for understanding about Lindy."

"Of course. Now come on. You've got a groom waiting."

"Okay, I'm ready."

She'd been ready three weeks ago, when Rick proposed. But it took a while to coordinate the family. She smiled to herself. That was one of the things a big family required—coordination. But finally, the big day had arrived.

She took her bouquet from her bed and examined herself in the mirror once more. She wanted so much to please Rick.

Walking down the stairs, she smiled at Will.

"You look beautiful, Vanessa. You're upholding the family honor quite well today."

"Thank you."

Then they walked to the door of the morning room. As the music changed to "The Wedding March," Vanessa looked at Rick for the first time that day. He was very handsome, but then, he always looked handsome to her. More important, he was a warm, giving man. Oh, she loved him.

Will led her down the aisle to Rick's side and she took his hand. The brief ceremony almost seemed like a dream. But when Rick kissed her at its end, she knew her dream was a reality. A beautiful reality.

With all the family there, and Dr. Cavanaugh and his wife, the house was almost full. But Rick wasn't interested in hanging around.

However, Vivian made a request before she'd let them leave. "I want a family portrait today. Please, may we do that?"

Of course they couldn't say no.

Vivian quickly arranged the family around them. Carrie stood with Jim, their two-week-old in her arms. David and Alex were next to them. On the other side, Rachel and J.D. and their little girl posed next to Jeff and Rebecca with their two children. Danny moved next to Will and Vivian, and Lindy stood beside the newlyweds.

The photographer didn't even need to tell them to smile. They were already glowing with happiness at being together.

After several photos and telling everyone goodbye, Rick took Vanessa aside. "I love your family, but I'm not interested in staying too long. You and I are going to spend two glorious weeks in Europe, just the two of us. Then we'll come home and be a part of your wonderful family. Do you agree?"

"Yes, especially the part about two glorious weeks in Europe."

"Glad to know we're in agreement, Mrs. Austin."

They departed amid the excited cheers of a large family that had come together because Vivian and Vanessa had loved them, and Will had found them.

And they would never be lost to each other again.

* * * * *

Watch for Judy Christenberry's upcoming story, KISS A RANDALL GOODBYE, coming October 2006 only from Harlequin American Romance.

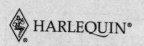

HARLEQUIN®

American ROMANCE®

COMING NEXT MONTH

#1121 THE WYOMING KID by Debbie Macomber

What do you get when you mix an ex-rodeo cowboy who is used to being *mobbed* by adoring fans, and a sweet schoolteacher who is *not* interested in him? For Lonnie Ellison, formerly the Wyoming Kid, Joy Fuller's lack of interest is infuriating—and very appealing. This could be a match made in heaven! *Don't miss this guest appearance by the beloved* New York Times *bestselling author!*

#1122 COWBOY M.D. by Pamela Britton

Alison Forester won't take no for an answer, especially not from Dr. Nicholas Sheppard, the renowned reconstructive surgeon. Ali's driven by personal reasons to make the new burn unit at her hospital a success. But Nick has issues of his own, and he'd rather patch up rodeo cowboys than join Ali. Even if she isn't your average hospital administrator.

#1123 TO CATCH A HUSBAND by Laura Marie Altom
U.S. Marshals

U.S. Marshal Charity Caldwell's biological clock is tick, tick, ticking away, but the man she's loved *forever* thinks of her as nothing more than a friend. Charity's about at her breaking point when she launches a plan to help Adam Logue think of her as more than a friend, and even more than a woman—it's a plan to make him see she'll be the perfect wife!

#1124 AARON UNDER CONSTRUCTION by Marin Thomas
The McKade Brothers

Life had been handed to Aaron McKade on a silver platter—until his grandfather dared the pampered heir to get his hands dirty and take a job building houses in the barrio of south central L.A. That's when he traded his Italian loafers for steel-toed boots—and found a boss lady with a tool belt to "rebuild" him....

www.eHarlequin.com

HARCNM0606

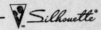

SPECIAL EDITION™

Welcome to Danbury Way—where nothing is as it seems...

Megan Schumacher has managed to maintain a low profile on Danbury Way by keeping the huge success of her graphics business a secret. But when a new client turns out to be a neighbor's sexy ex-husband, rumors of their developing romance quickly start to swirl.

THE RELUCTANT CINDERELLA

by CHRISTINE RIMMER

Available July 2006

Don't miss the first book from the Talk of the Neighborhood miniseries.

HOTEL MARCHAND

Four sisters.
A family legacy.
And someone is out to destroy it.

A captivating new limited continuity, launching June 2006

The most beautiful hotel in New Orleans,
and someone is out to destroy it. But mystery,
danger and some surprising family revelations
and discoveries won't stop the Marchand sisters
from protecting their birthright…
and finding love along the way.

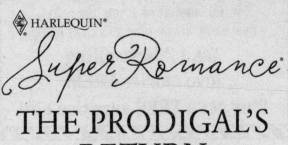

HARLEQUIN®
Super Romance®

THE PRODIGAL'S RETURN

by *Anna DeStefano*

Prom night for Jenn Gardner and Neal Cain turned into a tragedy that tore them apart. Eight years later, Jenn has made a life for herself and her young daughter. But when Neal comes home, Jenn sees that he is still consumed with the past. Maybe she can convince him that he's paid enough and deserves happiness a second time around.

"Anna DeStefano's remarkable stories of the healing power of love touch the heart with hope. One of the genre's rising stars..."
–Gayle Wilson, two-time
RITA® Award-winning author

On sale July 2006!
Available wherever books are sold, including most bookstores, supermarkets, discount stores and drugstores.

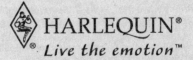

HARLEQUIN®
Live the emotion™